Marx Joyce
Hardy Austen
Defoe Abbott Emerson Hugo
Melville Machiavelli Cooper Chesterton Eliot
Stoker Montaigne Haggard Molière Grimm
Wilde Carroll Christie Maupassant Byron Schiller
Garnett Fitzgerald Engels Smith Kafka
Goethe Einstein Hawthorne Kipling Doyle Hall
Cotton Dostoyevsky Willis
Baum Henry Nietzsche
Leslie Dumas Flaubert Turgenev Balzac
Stockton Vatsyayana Crane
Burroughs Verne
Curtis Tocqueville Gogol Vinci
Homer Widger Tolstoy Whitman Busch
Darwin Thoreau Twain Scott
Potter Freud Zola Lawrence Plato Harte
Kant Jowett Stevenson Dickens Burton Hesse
Andersen Cervantes
London Descartes Voltaire
Poe Aristotle Wells
Hale James Hastings Cooke
Bunner Shakespeare Irving
Richter Chambers
Doré da Shaw Benedict Alcott
Dante Chekhov Wodehouse Pushkin
Swift Newton

 tredition®

tredition was established in 2006 by Sandra Latusseck and Soenke Schulz. Based in Hamburg, Germany, tredition offers publishing solutions to authors and publishing houses, combined with world-wide distribution of printed and digital book content. tredition is uniquely positioned to enable authors and publishing houses to create books on their own terms and without conventional manu-facturing risks.

For more information please visit: www.tredition.com

## TREDITION CLASSICS

This book is part of the TREDITION CLASSICS series. The creators of this series are united by passion for literature and driven by the intention of making all public domain books available in printed format again - worldwide. Most TREDITION CLASSICS titles have been out of print and off the bookstore shelves for decades. At tredition we believe that a great book never goes out of style and that its value is eternal. Several mostly non-profit literature projects provide content to tredition. To support their good work, tredition donates a portion of the proceeds from each sold copy. As a reader of a TREDITION CLASSICS book, you support our mission to save many of the amazing works of world literature from oblivion. See all available books at www.tredition.com.

## Project Gutenberg

The content for this book has been graciously provided by Project Gutenberg. Project Gutenberg is a non-profit organization founded by Michael Hart in 1971 at the University of Illinois. The mission of Project Gutenberg is simple: To encourage the creation and distribution of eBooks. Project Gutenberg is the first and largest collection of public domain eBooks.

# Addresses by the right reverend Phillips Brooks

Phillips Brooks

# Imprint

This book is part of TREDITION CLASSICS

Author: Phillips Brooks
Cover design: Buchgut, Berlin – Germany

Publisher: tredition GmbH, Hamburg - Germany
ISBN: 978-3-8424-7604-2

www.tredition.com
www.tredition.de

# CONTENTS.


I. THE BEAUTY OF A LIFE OF SERVICE 9

II. THOUGHT AND ACTION 34

III. THE DUTY OF THE CHRISTIAN BUSINESS MAN 63

IV. TRUE LIBERTY 88

V. THE CHRIST IN WHOM CHRISTIANS BELIEVE 110

VI. ABRAHAM LINCOLN 140

# I. THE BEAUTY OF A LIFE OF SERVICE.

I should like to read to you again the words of Jesus from the 8th chapter of the Gospel of St. John: —

> "Then said Jesus to those Jews which believed on Him, if ye continue in My word, then are ye My disciples indeed; and ye shall know the truth, and the truth shall make you free. They answered him, We be Abraham's seed, and were never in bondage to any man; how sayest Thou, ye shall be made free? Jesus answered them, Verily, verily, I say unto you, whosoever committeth sin is the servant of sin. And the servant abideth not in the house forever, but the Son abideth ever. If the Son, therefore, shall make you free, ye shall be free indeed."

I want to speak to you to-day about the purpose and the result of the freedom which Christ gives to His disciples and the freedom into which man enters when he fulfils his life. The purpose and result of freedom is service. It sounds to us at first like a contradiction, like a paradox. Great truths very often present themselves to us in the first place as paradoxes, and it is only when we come to combine the two different terms of which they are composed and see how it is only by their meeting that the truth does reveal itself to us, that the truth does become known. It is by this same truth that God frees our souls, not from service, not from duty, but into service and into duty, and he who makes mistakes the purpose of his freedom mistakes the character of his freedom. He who thinks that he is being released from the work, and not set free in order that he may accomplish that work, mistakes the Christ from whom the freedom comes, mistakes the condition into which his soul is invited to enter. For if I was right in saying what I said the other day, that the freedom of a man simply consists in the larger opportunity to be and to do all that God makes him in His creation capable of being and doing, then certainly if man has been capable of service it is only by the entrance into service, by the acceptance of that life of service for which God has given man the capacity, that he enters into the fulness of his freedom and becomes the liberated child of God. You remember what I said with regard to the manifestations of freedom and the figures and the illustrations, perhaps some of them which we used, of the way in which the bit of iron, taken out of its uselessness, its helplessness, and set in the midst of the great machine, thereby recognizes the purpose of its existence, and does the work for which it was appointed, for it immediately becomes the servant of the machine into which it was placed. Every part of its impulse flows through all of its substance, and it does the thing which it was made to do. When the ice has melted upon the plain it is only when it finds its way into the river and flows forth freely to do the work which the live water has to do that it really attains to its freedom. Only then is it really liberated from the bondage in which it was held while it was fastened in the chains of winter. The same freed ice waits until it so finds its freedom, and when man is set free simply into the enjoyment of his own life, simply into the realization of his own existence, he has not attained the purposes of his freedom, he has not come to the purposes of his life.

It is one of the signs to me of how human words are constantly becoming perverted that it surprises us when we think of freedom as a condition in which a man is called upon to do, and is enabled to do, the duty that God has laid upon him. Duty has become to us such a hard word, service has become to us a word so full of the spirit of bondage, that it surprises us at the first moment when we are called upon to realize that it is in itself a word of freedom. And yet we constantly are lowering the whole thought of our being, we are bringing down the greatness and richness of that with which we have to deal, until we recognize that God does not call us to our fullest life simply for ourselves. The spirit of selfishness is continually creeping in. I think it may almost be said that there has been no selfishness in the history of man like that which has exhibited itself in man's religious life, showing itself in the way in which man has seized upon spiritual privileges and rejoiced in the good things that are to come to him in the hereafter, because he had made himself the servant of God. The whole subject of selfishness, and the way in which it loses itself and finds itself again, is a very interesting one, and I wish that we had time to dwell upon it. It comes into a sort of general law which we are recognizing everywhere—the way in which a man very often, in his pursuit of the higher form of a condition in which he has been living, seems to lose that condition for a little while and only to reach it a little farther on. He seems to be abandoned by that power only that he may meet it by and by and enter more deeply into its heart and come more completely into its service. So it is, I think, with the self-devotion, consecration, and self-forgetfulness in which men realize their life. Very often in the lower stages of man's life he forgets himself, with a slightly emphasized individual existence, not thinking very much of the purpose of his life, till he easily forgets himself among the things that are around him and forgets himself simply because there is so little of himself for him to forget; but do not you know perfectly well how very often when a man's life becomes intensified and earnest, when he becomes completely possessed with some great passion and desire, it seems for the time to intensify his selfishness? It does intensify his selfishness. He is thinking so much in regard to himself that the thought of other persons and their interests is shut out of his life. And so very often when a man has set before him the great passion of the divine life, when he is called by God to live the life of God, and to enter into the rewards of God, very often there seems to close around his life a certain bondage of selfishness, and he who gave himself freely to his fellow-men before now seems, by the very intensity, eagerness, and earnestness with which his mind is set upon the prize of the new life which is presented to him—it seems as if everything became concentrated upon himself, the saving of his soul, the winning of his salvation. That seat in heaven seems to burn so before his eyes that he cannot be satisfied for a moment with any thought that draws him away from it, and he presses forward that he may be saved. But by and by, as he enters more deeply into that life, the self-forgetfulness comes to him again and as a diviner thing. By and by, as the man walks up the mountain, he seems to pass out of the cloud which hangs about the lower slopes of the mountain, until at last he stands upon the pinnacle at the top, and there is in the perfect light. Is it not exactly like the mountain at whose foot there seems to be the open sunshine where men see everything, and on whose summit there is the sunshine, but on whose sides, and half way up, there seems to linger a long cloud, in which man has to struggle until he comes to the full result of his life? So it is with self-consecration, with service. You easily do it in some small ways in the lower life. Life becomes intensified and earnest with a serious purpose, and it seems as if it gathered itself together into selfishness. Only then it opens by and by into the largest and noblest works of men, in which they most manifest the richness of their human nature and appropriate the strength of God. Those are great and unselfish acts. We know it at once if we turn to Him who represents the fulness of the nature of our humanity.

When I turn to Jesus and think of Him as the manifestation of His own Christianity—and if men would only look at the life of Jesus to see what Christianity is, and not at the life of the poor representatives of Jesus whom they see around them, there would be so much more clearness, they would be rid of so many difficulties and doubts. When I look at the life of Jesus I see that the purpose of consecration, of emancipation, is service of His fellow-men. I cannot think for a moment of Jesus as doing that which so many religious people think they are doing when they serve Christ, when they give their lives to Him. I cannot think of Him as simply saving His own soul, living His own life, and completing His own nature in the sight of God. It is a life of service from beginning to end. He gives himself to man because He is absolutely the Child of God, and He sets up service, and nothing but service, to be the ultimate purpose, the one great desire, on which the souls of His followers should be set, as His own soul is set, upon it continually.

What is it that Christ has left to be His symbol in the world, that we put upon our churches, what we wear upon our hearts, that stands forth so perpetually us the symbol of Christ's life? Is it a throne from which a ruler utters his decrees? Is it a mountain top upon which some rapt seer sits, communing with himself and with the voices around him, and gathering great truth into his soul and delighting in it? No, not the throne and not the mountain top. It is the cross. Oh, my brethren, that the cross should be the great symbol of our highest measure, that that which stands for consecration, that that which stands for the divine statement that a man does not live for himself and that a man loses himself when he does live for himself—that that should be the symbol of our religion and the great sign and token of our faith? What sort of Christians are we that go about asking for the things of this life first, thinking that it shall make us prosperous to be Christians, and then a little higher asking for the things that pertain to the eternal prosperity, when the Great Master, who leaves us the great law, in whom our Christian life is spiritually set forth, has as His great symbol the cross, the cross, the sign of consecration and obedience? It is not simply suffering too. Christ does not stand primarily for suffering. Suffering is an accident. It does not matter whether you and I suffer. "Not enjoyment and not sorrow" is our life, not sorrow any more than enjoyment, but obedience and duty. If duty brings sorrow, let it bring sorrow. It did bring sorrow to the Christ, because it was impossible for a man to serve the absolute righteousness in this world and not to sorrow. If it had brought joy, and glory, and triumph, if it had been greeted at its entrance and applauded on the way, He would have been as truly the consecrated soul that He was in the days when, over a road that was marked with the blood of His footprints, He found His way up at last to the torturing cross. It is not suffering; it is obedience. It is not pain; it is consecration of life. It is the joy of service that makes the life of Christ, and for us to serve Him, serving fellow-man and God — as he served fellow-man and God — whether it bring pain or joy, if we can only get out of our souls the thought that it matters not if we are happy or sorrowful, if only we are dutiful and faithful, and brave and strong, then we should be in the atmosphere, we should be in the great company of the Christ.

It surprises me very often when I hear good Christian people talk about Christ's entrance into this world, Christ's coming to save this world. They say it was so marvellous that Jesus should be willing to come down from His throne in heaven and undertake all the strange sorrow and distress that belonged to Him when He came to save the world from its sins. Wonderful? There was no wonder in it; no wonder if we enter up into the region where Jesus lives and think of life as He must have thought of life. It is the same wonder that people feel about the miracles of Jesus. Is it a wonder that when a divine life is among men, nature should have a response to make to Him, and He should do things that you and I, in our little humanity, find it impossible to do? No, indeed, there is no wonder that God loved the world. There is no wonder that Christ, the Son of God, at any sacrifice undertook to save the world. The wonder would have been if God, sitting in His heaven, the wonder would have been if Jesus, ready to come here to the earth and seeing how it was possible to save man from sin by suffering, had not suffered. Do you wonder at the mother, when she gives her life without a hesitation or a cry, when she gives her life with joy, with thankfulness, for her child, counting it her privilege? Do you wonder at the patriot, the hero, when he rushes into the battle to do the good deed which it is possible for him to do? No; read your own nature deeper and you will understand your Christ. It is no wonder that He should have died upon the cross; the wonder would have been if, with the inestimable privilege of saving man, He had shrunk from that cross and turned away. It sets before us that it is not the glories of suffering, it is not the necessity of suffering, it is simply the beauty of obedience and the fulfilment of a man's life in doing his duty and rendering the service which it is possible for him to render to his fellow-man.

I said that a man when he did that left behind him all the thought of the life which he was willing to live within himself, even all the highest thought. It is not your business and mine to study whether we shall get to heaven, even to study whether we shall be good men; it is our business to study how we shall come into the midst of the purposes of God and have the unspeakable privilege in these few years of doing something of His work. And yet so is our life all one, so is the kingdom of God which surrounds us and infolds us one bright and blessed unity, that when a man has devoted himself to the service of God and his fellow-man, immediately he is thrown back upon his own nature, and he sees now — it is the right place for him to see — that he must be the brave, strong, faithful man, because it is impossible for him to do his duty and to render his service, except it is rendered out of a heart that is full of faithfulness, that is brave and true. There is one word of Jesus that always comes back to me as about the noblest thing that human lips have ever said upon our earth, and the most comprehensive thing, that seems to sweep into itself all the commonplace experience of mankind. Do you remember when He was sitting with His disciples, at the last supper, how He lifted up His voice and prayed, and in the midst of His prayer there came these wondrous words: "For their sakes I sanctify myself, that they also might be sanctified"? The whole of human life is there. Shall a man cultivate himself? No, not primarily. Shall a man serve the world, strive to increase the kingdom of God in the world? Yes, indeed, he shall. How shall he do it? By cultivating himself, and instantly he is thrown back upon his own life. "For their sakes I sanctify myself, that they also might be sanctified." I am my best, not simply for myself, but for the world. My brethren, is there anything in all the teachings that man has had from his fellow-man, all that has come down to him from the lips of God, that is nobler, that is more far-reaching than that—to be my best not simply for my own sake, but for the sake of the world into which, setting my best, I shall make that world more complete, I shall do my little part to renew and to recreate it in the image of God? That is the law of my existence. And the man that makes that the law of his existence neither neglects himself nor his fellow-men, neither becomes the self-absorbed student and cultivator of his own life upon the one hand, nor does he become, abandoning himself, simply the wasting benefactor of his brethren upon the other. You can help your fellow-men: you must help your fellow-men; but the only way you can help them is by being the noblest and the best man that it is possible for you to be. I watch the workman build upon the building which by and by is to soar into the skies, to toss its pinnacles up to the heaven, and I see him looking up and wondering where those pinnacles are to be, thinking how high they are to be, measuring the feet, wondering how they are to be built, and all the time he is cramming a rotten stone into the building just where he has set to work. Let him forget the pinnacles, if he will, or hold only the floating image of them in his imagination for his inspiration; but the thing that he must do is to put a brave, strong soul, an honest and substantial life into the building just where he is now at work.

It seems to me that that comes home to us all. Men are questioning now as they never have questioned before whether Christianity is indeed the true religion which is to be the salvation of the world. They are feeling how the world needs salvation, how it needs regeneration, how it is wrong and bad all through and through, mixed with the good that is in it everywhere. Everywhere there is the good and the bad, and the great question that is on men's minds to-day, as I believe it has never been upon men's minds before, is this: Is this Christian religion, with its high pretensions, this Christian life that claims so much for itself, is it competent for the task that it has undertaken to do? Can it meet all these human problems, and relieve all these human miseries, and fulfil all these human hopes? It is the old story over again, when John the Baptist, puzzled in his prison, said to Jesus, "Art thou He that should come? or look we for another?" It seems to me that the Christian Church is hearing that cry in its ears to-day: "Art thou He that should come?" Can you do this which the world unmistakably needs to be done?

Christian men, it is for us to give our bit of answer to that question. It is for us, in whom the Christian Church is at this moment partially embodied, to declare that Christianity, that the Christian faith, the Christian manhood, can do that for the world which the world needs. You say, "What can I do?" You can furnish one Christian life. You can furnish a life so faithful to every duty, so ready for every service, so determined not to commit every sin, that the great Christian Church shall be the stronger for your living in it, and the problem of the world be answered, and a certain great peace come into this poor, perplexed phase of our humanity as it sees that new revelation of what Christianity is. Yes, Christ can give the world the thing it needs in unknown ways and methods that we have not yet begun to suspect. Christianity has not yet been tried. My friends, no man dares to condemn the Christian faith to-day, because the Christian faith has not been tried. Not until men get rid of the thought that it is a poor machine, an expedient for saving them from suffering and pain, not until they get the grand idea of it as the great power of God present in and through the lives of men, not until then does Christianity enter upon its true trial and become ready to show what it can do. Therefore we struggle against our sin in order that men may be saved around us, and not simply that our own souls may be saved.

Tell me you have a sin that you mean to commit this evening that is going to make this night black. What can keep you from committing that sin? Suppose you look into its consequences. Suppose the wise man tells you what will be the physical consequences of that sin. You shudder and you shrink, and, perhaps, you are partially deterred. Suppose you see the; glory that might come to you, physical, temporal, spiritual, if you do not commit that sin. The opposite of it shows itself to you—the blessing and the richness in your life. Again there comes a great power that shall control your lust and wickedness. Suppose there comes to you something even deeper than that, no consequence on consequence at all, but simply an abhorrence for the thing, so that your whole nature shrinks from it as the nature of God shrinks from a sin that is polluting and filthy and corrupt and evil. They are all great powers. Let us thank God for them all. He knows that we are weak enough to need every power that can possibly be brought to bear upon our feeble lives; but if, along with all of them, there could come this other power, if along with them there could come the certainty that if you refrain from that sin to-night you make the sum of sin that is in the world, and so the sum of all temptation that is in the world, and so the sum of future evil that is to spring out of temptation in the world, less, shall there not be a nobler impulse rise up in your heart, and shall you not say: "I will not do it; I will be honest, I will be sober, I will be pure, at least, to-night"? I dare to think that there are men here to whom that appeal can come, men who, perhaps, will be all dull and deaf if one speaks to them about their personal salvation; who, if one dares to picture to them, appealing to their better nature, trusting to their nobler soul, that there is in them the power to save other men from sin, and to help the work of God by the control of their own passions and the fulfilment of their own duty, will be stirred to the higher life. Men—very often we do not trust them enough—will answer to the higher appeal that seems to be beyond them when the poor, lower appeal that comes within the region of their selfishness is cast aside, and they will have nothing to do with it.

Oh, this marvellous, this awful power that we have over other people's lives! Oh! the power of the sin that you have done years and years ago! It is awful to think of it. I think there is hardly anything more terrible to the human thought than this—the picture of a man who, having sinned years and years ago in a way that involved other souls in his sin, and then, having repented of his sin and undertaken another life, knows certainly that the power, the consequence of that sin is going on outside of his reach, beyond even his ken and knowledge. He cannot touch it. You wronged a soul ten years ago. You taught a boy how to tell his first mercantile lie; you degraded the early standards of his youth. What has become of that boy to-day? You may have repented. He has passed put of your sight. He has gone years and years ago. Somewhere in this great, multitudinous mass of humanity he is sinning and sinning and reduplicating and extending the sin that you did. You touched the faith of some believing soul years ago with some miserable sneer of yours, with some cynical and sceptical disparagement of God and of the man who is the utterance of God upon the earth. You taught the soul that was enthusiastic to be full of scepticisms and doubts. You wronged a woman years ago, and her life has gone out from your life, you cannot begin to tell where. You have repented of your sin. You have bowed yourself, it may be, in dust and ashes. You have entered upon a new life. You are pure to-day. But where is the sceptical soul? Where is the ruined woman whom you sent forth into the world out of the shadow of your sin years ago? You cannot touch that life. You cannot reach it. You do not know where it is. No steps of yours, quickened with all your earnestness, can pursue it. No contrition of yours can drawback its consequences. Remorse cannot force the bullet back again into the gun from which it once has gone forth. It makes life awful to the man who has ever sinned, who has ever wronged and hurt another life because of this sin, because no sin ever was done that did not hurt another life. I know the mercy of our God, that while He has put us into each other's power to a fearful extent, He never will let any soul absolutely go to everlasting ruin for another's sin; and so I dare to see the love of God pursuing that lost soul where you cannot pursue it. But that does not for one moment lift the shadow from your heart, or cease to make you tremble when you think of how your sin has outgrown itself and is running far, far away where you can never follow it.

Thank God the other thing is true as well. Thank God that when a man does a bit of service, however little it may be, of that too he can never trace the consequences. Thank God that that which in some better moment, in some nobler inspiration, you did ten years ago to make your brother's faith a little more strong, to let your shop boy confirm and not doubt the confidence in man which he had brought into his business, to establish the purity of a soul instead of staining it and shaking it, thank God, in this quick, electric atmosphere in which we live, that, too, runs forth. Do not say in your terror, "I will do nothing." You must do something. Only let Christ tell you—let

Christ tell you that there is nothing that a man rests upon in the moment, that he thinks of, as he looks back upon it when it has sunk into the past, with any satisfaction, except some service to his fellow-man, some strengthening and helping of a human soul.

Two men are walking down the street together and talking away. See what different conditions those two men are in. One of them has his soul absolutely full of the desire to help his fellow-man. He peers into those faces as he goes, and sees the divine possibility that is in them, and he sees the divine nature everywhere. They are talking about the idlest trifles, about the last bit of local Boston politics. But in their souls one of those men has consecrated himself, with the new morning, to the glorious service of God, and the other of them is asking how he may be a little richer in his miserable wealth when the day sinks. Oh, we look into the other world and read the great words and hear it said, Between me and thee, this and that, there is a great gulf fixed; and we think of something that is to come in the eternal life. Is there any gulf in eternity, is there any gulf between heaven and hell that is wider, and deeper, and blacker, that is more impassable than that gulf which lies between these two men going upon their daily way? Oh, friends, it is not that God is going to judge us some day. That is not the awful thing. It is that God knows us now. If I stop an instant and know that God knows me through all these misconceptions and blunders of my brethren, that God knows me — that is the awful thing. The future judgment shall but tell it. It is here, here upon my conscience, now. It is awful to think how the commonplace things that men can do, the commonplace thoughts that men can think, the commonplace lives that men can live, are but in the bosom of the future. The thing that impresses me more and more is this — that we only need to have extended to the multitude that which is at this moment present in the few, and the world really would be saved. There is but the need of the extension into a multitude of souls of that which a few souls have already attained in their consecration of themselves to human good, and to the service of God, and I will not say the millennium would have come, I don't know much about the millennium, but heaven would have come, the new Jerusalem would be here. There are men enough in this church this morning, there are men enough sitting here within the sound of my voice to-day, if they were inspired by the spirit of God and counted it the great privilege of their life, to do the work of God—there are men enough here to save this city, and to make this a glowing city of our Lord, to relieve its poverty, to lighten its darkness, to lift up the cloud that is upon hearts, to turn it into a great, I will not say psalm-singing city, but God-serving, God-abiding city, to touch all the difficult problems of how society and government ought to be organized then with a power with which they should yield their difficulty and open gradually. The light to measure would be clear enough, if only the spirit is there. Give me five hundred men, nay, give me one hundred men of the spirit that I know to-day in three men that I well understand, and I will answer for it that the city shall be saved. And you, my friend, are one of the five hundred—you are one of the one hundred.

"Oh, but," you say, "is not this slavery over again? You have talked about freedom, and here I am once more a slave. I had about got free from the bondage of my fellow-men, and here I am right in the midst of it again. What has become of my personality, of my independence, if I am to live thus?" Ay, you have got to learn what every noblest man has always learned, that no man becomes independent of his fellow-men excepting in serving his fellow-men. You have got to learn that Christianity comes to us not simply as a luxury but as a force, and no man who values Christianity simply as a luxury which he possesses really gets the Christianity which he tries to value. Only when Christianity is a force, only when I seek independence of men in serving men, do I cease to be a slave to their whims. I must dress as they think I ought to dress; I must walk in the streets as they think I ought to walk; I must do business just after their fashion; I must accept their standards; but when Christ has taken possession of me and I am a total man, I am more or less independent of these men. Shall I care about their little whims and oddities? Shall I care about how they criticise the outside of my life? Shall I peer into their faces as I meet them in the street, to see whether they approve of me or not? And yet am I not their servant? There is nothing now I will not do to serve them, there is nothing now I will not do to save them. If the cross comes, I welcome the cross, and look upon it with joy, if, by my death upon the cross in any way, I may echo the salvation of my Lord and save them. Independent of them? Surely. And yet their servant? Perfectly. Was ever man so independent in Jerusalem as Jesus was? What cared He for the sneer of the Pharisee, for the learned scorn of the Sadducee, for the taunt of the people and the little boys that had been taught to jeer at Him as He went down the street, and yet the very servant of all their life? He says there are two kinds of men—they who sit upon a throne and eat, and they who serve. "I am among you as he that serveth." Oh, seek independence. Insist upon independence. Insist that you will not be the slave of the poor, petty standards of your fellow-men. But insist upon it only in the way in which it can be insisted upon, by becoming absolutely the servant of their needs. So only shall you be independent of their whims. There is one great figure, and it has taken in all Christian consciousness, that again and again this work with Christ has been asserted to be the true service in the army of a great master, of a great captain, who goes before us to his victory, that it is asserted that in that captain, in the entrance into his army, every power is set free. Do you remember the words that a good many of us read or heard yesterday in our churches, where Jesus was doing one of His miracles, and it is said that a devil was cast out, the dumb spake? Every power becomes the man's possession, and he uses it in his freedom, and he fights with it with all his force, just as soon as the devil is cast out of him.

I have tried to tell you the noblest motive in which you should be a pure, an upright, a faithful, and a strong man. It is not for the salvation of your life, it is not for the salvation of yourself. It is not for the satisfaction of your tastes. It is that you may take your place in the great army of God and go forward having something to do with the work that He is doing in the world. You remember the days of the war, and how ashamed of himself a man felt who never touched with his finger the great struggle in which the nation was engaged. Oh, to go through this life and never touch with my finger the vast work that Christ is doing, and when the cry of triumph arises at the end to stand there, not having done one little, unknown, unnoticed thing to bring about that which is the true life of the man and of the world, that is awful. And I dare to believe that there are young men in this church this morning who, failing to be touched by every promise of their own salvation and every threatening of their own damnation, will still lift themselves up and take upon them the duty of men, and be soldiers of Jesus Christ, and have a part in the battle, and have a part somewhere in the victory that is sure to come. Don't be selfish anywhere. Don't be selfish, most of all, in your religion. Let yourselves free into your religion, and be utterly unselfish. Claim your freedom in service.

# II. THOUGHT AND ACTION.

I want once more to read to you these words from the eighth chapter of the Gospel of St. John:

> "As He spake these words, many believed on Him. Then said Jesus to those Jews which believed on Him, If ye continue in My word, then are ye My disciples indeed; And ye shall know the truth, and the truth shall make you free. They answered Him, We be Abraham's seed, and were never in bondage to any man: how sayest Thou, Ye shall be made free? Jesus answered them, Verily, verily, I say unto you, Whosoever committeth sin is the servant of sin. And the servant abideth not in the house for ever: but the Son abideth ever. If the Son therefore shall make you free, ye shall be free indeed."

There are two great regions in which the life of every true man resides. They are the region of action and the region of thought. It is impossible to separate these two regions from one another and to bid one man live in one of them alone and the other man live only in the other of them. It is impossible to say to the business man that he shall live only in the region of action, it is impossible to say to the scholar that he shall live only in the region of thought, for thought and action make one complete and single life. Thought is not simply the sea upon which the world of action rests, but, like the air which pervades the whole solid substance of our globe, it permeates and fills it in every part. It is thought which gives to it its life. It is thought which makes the manifestation of itself in every different action of man. I hope we are not so deluded as men have been sometimes, as some men are to-day, that we shall try to separate these two lives from one another, and one man say, "Everything depends upon my action, and I care not what I think," or, as men have said, at least, in other times, "If I think right, it matters not how

I act." But the right thought and the right action make one complete and single man.

Now we have been speaking, upon these Monday noons, with regard to the freedom of that highest life which is lived under the inspiration of Jesus Christ and which we call the Christian life. We have claimed that it is the highest of all lives because it is the freest of all lives, that it is the freest of all lives because it is the highest, and it may be that we have thought that it was true with regard to the active life in which men live, it may be that we have somehow persuaded ourselves, that it has seemed to us as if there were evidence that a man who lived his life in the following of Jesus Christ was a free man in regard to his activity. But now there comes to us the other thought, and it is impossible for us to meet together as we have met together again and again here without asking with regard to the other region of man's life and how it is with man there, for there are a great many people, I believe, who think that while the Christian faith offers to man a noble sphere of action and sets free powers that would otherwise remain unchanged, yet when we come to the region of thought or belief, there it is inevitable that man should know himself, when he accepts the faith of Jesus Christ, it is inevitable that there the man should become less free than it has been thought that he was before the blessed Saviour was accepted as the Master and the ruler of his life. Men say to themselves and to one another, "Yes, I shall be freer to act, I shall be nobler in my action, but I shall certainly enchain mind and spirit, I shall certainty bind myself to think, away from the rich freedom of thought in which I have been inclined to live." We make very much of free thought in these days. Let us always remember that free thought means the opportunity to think, and not the opportunity not to think. We rejoice in the way in which our fathers came to this country and in their children perpetuated the purpose of their coming, in order that they might have freedom to worship God. Do we worship God? Simply to have attained freedom and not to use freedom for its true purpose, not to live within the world of freedom according to the life which is given to us there—that is to do dishonor to the freedom, to disown the purpose for which the freedom has been given to us. I want to speak to you then, while I may speak to-day, with regard to the freedom of the Christian thought.

I want to claim, that which I believe with all my soul, that he who lives in the faith of Jesus Christ lives in the freest action of his mental powers, and there sees before him and makes himself a part of the large world into which man shall enter, in which he has perfect liberty and can exercise his powers as he could never have exercised them without. It is not very strange to think that men should have sometimes come to think that the religion of Jesus Christ was a slavery that was laid upon the mind of man, because very often those who have been the disciples of that religion, those who have been the preachers and exponents of that religion, have claimed just exactly that thing. They have seemed to say to themselves and to one another, to the world to which they speak, that man does give up the powers of his reason when he enters into the powers of his faith, when he enters into the great realm of faith. Led by some sort of influence, led by some heresy with regard to the capacity of man, or with regard to the dealing of God with man, or with regard to the purposes of man's life upon the earth, they have been content to say that man must give up the power of thought in order that he might enter into the Christian life and attain to all the purposes of the Christian discipline, they have been content to say that man must give up the noblest power of his nature in order to enter upon the highest life. Well might a man hesitate, hesitate whatever the blessings that were offered to him in the fulness of the Christian experience, if he were called upon to give up that which made the very centre and glory of his life, that which linked him most immediately to the God from whom he sprang. It would be as if in the storm the ship should cast over its engine in order to save its own life. The ship might be saved a little while from going down in the depths of despair, but it never would reach the port to which it had been bound; it never would accomplish the purpose of the voyage upon which it had set forth. Let us put absolutely away from, us all such thoughts. Let us come under the inspiration of Jesus Christ Himself, who says to us, in these words which we have repeatedly read to one another, that it is the truth that is to make us free, and that the entrance of the man therefore into that freedom is the largest freedom, of every region of man's life.

I want to speak to you of the way in which my Master, Jesus Christ, appeals to the intelligence of man, of the way in which He comes to us in the noblest part of our nature, and claims us there for our true life within Himself. I would feel altogether wrong if I let you depart, if I allowed you to meet here with me week after week and say these words which I am privileged to speak to you unless I did thus claim that the Christian life is the largest life of the human intellect, that in it the noblest and central powers of man shall attain to their true liberty. It is given for us perhaps to ask ourselves for one moment why it is that man thinks, is ready to think, that he must give up the very noblest part of his life, his powers of thinking, in order that he may enter into Christianity. It seems to me that there are certain reasons for it which we can see; but how fallacious those reasons are! Is it not partly because man, when he is called upon to live Jesus' life, when he is called upon to be a spiritual creature, immediately sees that he is entering into a new and different region from that in which his reason has always been exercised. He has been dealing with those things that belong to this earth, with the different duties and opportunities and pleasures that present themselves to him every day, and that higher and loftier region into which he has entered seems to have no capacity to call forth those powers which he has been using in this lower region. And then I think again there is upon the souls of men who deal with Christianity one great conviction which is very deep and strong. It is that the Christian religion cannot be absolutely that which it presents itself to human mankind as being, because it is so rich in the blessings that it offers, because it comes with such a large enjoyment to our human life, and opens such great opportunities for human living. Is it not because it seems to us too good to be true that we sometimes turn away from Christianity, and think that if we enter it at all we must enter it in the dark, that it cannot possibly appeal to these human natures and make them understand its truth, and let them take it into their intelligence that thence it may issue into the soul and become the guiding power of the life? Sometimes it seems as if Christianity were so high that it was impossible that man should attain to it, as if it were something altogether beyond our human powers. Do you want me, a creature with this human body and this human relationship, with this body and with these perpetual bindings and connections with my fellow-men, do you want me to mount up and live among the stars and hold communion with the God of all? And if you want me to, is there any possibility of my doing it? Such a life is glorious, but not for me. It goes beyond any capacity that I possess. Ask yourselves, my friends, if something like this which I have tried to describe is not very often in your minds as you hear the magnificent invitations which Christ gives to the human soul to live its fullest life, to man to be his fullest being. There are, no doubt, other reasons which present themselves to men, and of those I do not speak. I will not think that the men who are listening here to me now, in a base and low way shrink from the evidence of Christianity and from the life of Christ because they do not want to enter into that religion because it would make too great demands upon them in the sacrifices that they would be called upon to make. It is said sometimes, and I doubt not that it is sometimes true, that men will not see the power and truth of Christianity because they do not want to see it. It seems to me that the other is also often true, and it is that upon which we would much rather dwell. Men sometimes hesitate at Christianity and tremble, and will not enter into the great region that is open to them, because they do not want it so intimately. The critical, the sceptical disposition is very often born just of man's perception of the glory of the life that is offered to him, and of the intense desire that is at the bottom of his soul to enter into that life. Who is the man that criticises the ship most carefully as she lies at the wharf, that will see what capacity she has for the great voyage that she has set before her? Is he the man who means to linger carelessly upon the bank and never sail away, or the man who is obliged, if she can sail across the ocean, to go with her? Just in proportion to the depth of interest with which we look upon all Christian truth we must be deep questioners with regard to the truth of that truth. We must search into all its evidence. We must try to understand how it commends itself to all our minds. But first of all we want to know certainly what Christianity is, if it is able to deal with the thing with which we are puzzling or never to give an intelligent definition of it.

How is it now? I go to a certain man and ask him, "Why do you not believe in Christianity?" and he says, "It is incredible. I cannot believe in it." "What is it that you cannot believe in?" and then he takes forsooth some little point of Christian doctrine, some speculation of some Christian teacher, some dogma of some Christian church, and says, "That is incredible," as if that were Christianity.

Over and over again men are telling that they do not believe in Christianity, when the real thing that they do not believe in is something that is no essential part of Christian faith whatsoever. They never have given to themselves a real definition of what the Christ and the Christianity in which they are called upon to believe, into which they are invited to enter, really is. The lecturer goes up and down the land and in the face of mighty audiences he denounces Christianity. He declares it to be unintelligible and absurd, to be monstrous and brutal. And when you ask what it is that he is thus denouncing, what it is that he is thus convicting over and over again, you find that it is something not simply which makes no part of Christianity, but which is absolutely hostile to the spirit of Christianity itself. Many and many a sceptical lecturer is denouncing that which Christian men would, with all their hearts, denounce; is declaring that to be untrue which no true Christian thinker really believes, that which is no real part of the great Christian faith, which is our glory. Do not think when I speak thus, when I say that there are things attached to Christianity which men do not believe, that they do not believe in the great truth of Jesus, without them, which men denouncing think that they are denouncing the religion which is saving the world. Do not think that I am simply paring away our great Christian faith, and making it mean just as little as possible in order that men may accept it into their lives. I am coming to the heart and soul of it. I want to know, if my life is all bound up with this religion of Jesus Christ, I want to know intrinsically what that religion is. I will scatter a thousand things which in the devout thought of men have fastened themselves to it. It is but clearing the ship for action, the making it ready that it may do its work, the binding everything tight just before the storm comes on, for that is just the moment when nothing essential to the ship itself must be cast away, when I make sure, if I can, that every plank and timber, that every iron and brass is in its true place and ready for the strain that may be put upon it.

But what, then, is the Christian religion? It is the simple following of the divine person, Jesus Christ, who, entering into our humanity, has made evident two things—the love of God for that humanity, and the power of that humanity to answer to the love of God. The one thing that the eye of the Christian sees and never can lose is that majestic, simple figure, great in its simplicity, in its innocence, in its purity and in its unworldliness, that walked once on this earth and that walks forever through the lives of men, showing Himself to human kind, manifest in human kind. The power to receive it, the divine life wakened in every child of man by the divine life manifested in Jesus Christ. That is the great Christian faith, and the man becomes a Christian in his belief when he assures himself that that manifestation of the divine life has been made and is perpetually being made, and he answers to that appeal of the Christ. He manifests his belief in action when he gives himself to the education and the guiding of that Christ, that in him there may be awakened the life of divinity, which is his true human life. Is it not glorious, this absolute simplicity of the Christian faith? It is not primarily a truth; it is a person, it is He who walked in Galilee and Judea, who sat in the houses of mankind, who hung upon the cross, in order that He might perfectly manifest how God could live and how man could suffer in the obedience to the life of God, and then sent forth out of that inspiration and said, "Lo, I am with you always, doing this very thing, being this very Saviour, even to the end of the world." That which the Christian man believes to-day as a Christian, whatever else he may believe in his private speculation, in his personal opinion, is this: The life of God manifest in Jesus of Nazareth and thenceforth going out into the world wakening the divine capacity in every man.

You say, "How can a man believe that? What evidence is there of it?" The personal evidence of Jesus Christ himself. It is the self testimony of Christ that makes the assurance of the Christian faith. Does that sound to you all unreasonable? Do you turn here in your pew or in your aisle and say, "After all, it is the old story which I have tested and know to be untrue."

Suppose yourself back there in Jerusalem. Suppose the self testimony came to you from the very person of Jesus Christ. Suppose the words that He absolutely said and the deeds that He absolutely did bore to you a testimony that some greater than a human life was there, and that then, as you pressed close to Him and became a part of His life, you found your own life awakened and became a nobler man, ashamed to sin, aspiring after holiness, thinking noble thoughts, lifting yourself not above the earth, but lifting yourself with the whole great earth, which then is taken up into the presence of God and made sacred through and through. I know no man in whom I trust except by the personal evidence that he bears to me of himself. I know no man's nature finally but by that testimony which the nature gives me of him. Bring me all evidence that the man is trustworthy, and then when I am convinced I will go and stand in the presence of that man himself, and he shall tell me. So the world stood, so the world stands to-day in the presence of Jesus Christ. His presence on earth is an historic fact. The words that He spoke are written down in a true record. The deeds that He did are the history of the manifestations of His character, and the story of His christendom is the continued manifestation of His life, the divine life in the life of man, made divine through Him. Now, a question that comes in the Christian's mind is "Why don't people believe this?" Why should they not? Is it not written in the historical record? Has it not manifested itself in the experience of mankind? If it has, surely then it appeals to man's reason, and is not merely the act of the blind, stupid thing which we call faith, but it is the noblest action of that hour in which I believe, in the heavens above me and in the earth under my feet, in the brother with whom I have to do in the long course of history, in the total humanity which has grandly lived. The reason that men do not believe it is that of course there seems to be to them some strange and previous presumption with regard to it, something which makes the story incredible. They say it is the supernatural in it, that it goes beyond the ordinary experience of man. Ah! it seems also strange to me, the ordinary experience of man. Who dares to dream that human life has lived its completest and shown the noblest power of receiving God into itself? Who dares to think that these few thousand years have exhausted this majestic and mysterious being that we call man? Who dares to think of his own life that, in these few thirty, forty, fifty years that he has lived, he has known and shown all that God can do in and for him? Who dares to say that it is impossible, that it is improbable, that he who is the child of God shall receive some newer and closer access to his father, that there shall come some new revelation which shall be written not in a book, not upon the skies, not in the history of human kind, not on the rocks under our feet, but here in our human flesh, that there shall be an incarnation, that the God who is perpetually trying to manifest Himself to human kind should find at last, should take at last the most exquisite, the most sensitive, the most perfect, the most divine of all material on which to write His message, and in that human nature show at once what God was and what man is? Until there be some exhaustive sight of human nature as that, it is in no wise improbable that there would be that which outgoes our observation, that once in the long music of our human life the great key-note of humanity shall be struck, that once in our great groping after the God who made us He shall seem to draw the veil aside, nay, more than that, shall come and like the sunlight crowd Himself through every cloud until He takes possession of our humanity.

"Ay," but you say, "those miracles in the life of Jesus Christ, how strange those are; how strange that He should have touched the water and the water become wine; how strange that He should have called to the dead man and he should have come forth from the tomb; how strange that He should have spoken to the waters and the storm grow still!" Ah, my friends, it seems to me that there again we are dishonoring nature as just before we did dishonor man. There again we are thinking that we have exhausted the capacity of this wondrous world in which we live. What is the glory of that world? That it answers to human kind. In the mystic tradition of the Book of Genesis it is told how, when God first made man, He set him master of this world and all its powers; and, ever since, the world has been answering to man, who is its master, and every message that comes back to him, every response that the field makes to the farmer, or that the rock makes to the scientist, is but an assertion and the culmination and the fulfilment of that which God did back there. As man has been, so has the world responded to his touch and call. Suppose that to-morrow morning the perfect man should come, not the man simply of the twentieth century or of the twenty-first, who shall be greater in his humanity than we, but suppose the perfect man, the perfect man because the divine man, comes. I cannot dream that nature shall not have words to say and a response to make to him that it will not make to these poor hands of mine. I can do something with the rock and field, I can do something with the sea and sky. What shall he do who is to my humanity what the perfect is to the absolutely and dreadfully imperfect? What shall the divine man do? When Paul speaks in that great verse of his and tells us how the whole creation groaneth and travaileth waiting for the manifestation of the Son of God, the whole future history of human science, of man's knowledge and use of the world, is in his words. The world shall know man as fast as man shows himself, and when the Son of God shall be manifested, then the groaning and travailing creation shall set all its powers free, and with the knowledge with which it floods him and with the usages and service with which it supplies him, it shall claim at last its glory as the servant, the obedient servant of man. The Son of man has come. You may at least suppose it if you do not believe it. And if He came to-morrow morning, would not this whole world lift itself up and answer Him? Who can say what the hills and valleys and trees and oceans and seas would have to say to Him who at last manifested that which the world had been waiting and groaning for, the manifestation, the complete manifestation, of the Son of God? That is the reason why I claim that miracles—I do not know that there have not been fastened upon the miraculous power of Jesus stories of things, thinking that they were done miraculously, which He did by what we choose in our ignorance to call the ordinary powers of nature—but I do know that the coming into the world must have been more to this world, that it would have been the most unnatural and incredible thing if the divine man coming here had been to the world and the world had been to him only what it is to us.

And now the question comes to each one of us—for I must hasten on—how shall a man get within the region of that which perhaps you recognize, which I do not see how you can help believing, how shall a man get within the region of that higher power and let it be the rule of his life, let it manifest itself through him? How do you get within the power of any force, my friends? Here is Christ, a force if He is anything, not a spectacle, not a miracle, not a marvel, not wonderful to look at, but a force to feel. How do you get within the power of any force? You look out of your window, and men say the frost is freezing, and you see your neighbors wrapping their cloaks about them and going down the street as if they were cold. Men say that a storm is blowing, and you see them shelter themselves against the storm that blows. How will you make that storm a true thing for yourself? Go out into it. Let the frost smite your cheek, let the rain beat into your face, let the wind blow upon your back, and then you know by personal experience what you had known by your observation before. And so I say that only when a man puts himself where he can feel the power of the Christ, where it is possible for him, if there be a Christ, if Christ be all that the Christian religion claims that He is, only when a man puts himself where he needs and must have and must certainly feel that Christ, if there be a Christ, only then has he a right to disbelieve if the Christ be not there, only then has he a right to believe if the Christ find him there. And where is that? When a man takes up the highest duties, when he accepts the noblest life, when he lays open his soul to the great exactions and obligations which belong to him in his spiritual nature, when he tries to be a pure man, a devoted man, a noble man, only then has he a chance to know that force which only then comes into its activity. Only when a man tries to live the divine life can the divine Christ manifest Himself to him. Therefore the true way for you to find Christ is not to go groping in a thousand books. It is not for you to try evidences about a thousand things that people have believed of Him, but it is for you to undertake so great a life, so devoted a life, so pure a life, so serviceable a life, that you cannot do it except by Christ, and then see whether Christ helps you. See whether there comes to you the certainty that you are a child of God, and the manifestation of the child of God becomes the most credible, the most certain thing to you in all of history.

It may have been that such moments have been in some of your lives. Think of the noblest moment that you ever passed, of the time when, lifted up to the heights of glory, or bowed down into the very depths of sorrow, every power that was in you was called forth to meet the exigency or to do the work. Think of the time when you stood upon the mountain top or plunged into the gulf. Remember that time—it may have been the death of your little child, it may have been your own sickness, it may have been your failure in business, it may have been the moment of your complete success in business, when you were solemnized as the great shower of wealth poured down upon you, and you felt that now you really had some work for God to do in the world. Ah, look back to that moment and see if then it seemed so strange to you that God should come into the presence and person of His universe, of His children, and take possession of their life. We grow so easily to forget our noblest and most splendid times. It seems to me there is no maxim for a noble life like this: Count always your highest moments your truest moments. Believe that in the time when you were the greatest and most spiritual man, then you were your truest self. Men do just the other thing. They say it was "an exception, a derangement of my nature, an exultation, a frenzy, it was something that I must not expect again." How about the time when they plunged into baseness and made their soul like a dog's soul? They shudder at the thought of that because they think it would come again. Nay, nay, shudder if you will at the thought of that, but believe that the highest you ever have been you may be all the time, and vastly higher still if only the power of the Christ can occupy you and fill your life all the time.

I said that there were many things that people attached to Christianity that did not belong to Christianity. I know there are. It is impossible that a great system like the system of Christ, a great person like the great person of Christ, should be in the world, and men not have speculated and thought in regard to Him. Those are not Christianity. I want to-day, if I may do nothing else, to tell you absolutely how simple and single the Christian faith, the Christ, really is. It is not the inspiration of this book or any theory in regard to its inspiration. It is not the election of certain souls and the perdition of other souls. It is not the length of man's punishment, whether it is going to be forever and ever, or whether man is to go to his restoration. It is not even the constitution of the divine life, the great truth of the way in which God lives within His own nature. None of these are the essence of the Christian faith, but simply this: The testimony of the divine in man to the divine in man that lifts the man up and says: "For me to be brutal is unmanly; to be divine is to be my only true self." Why do I believe in God? If some man asked me, when on the street, I think I should have an answer to give him. I could give one great reason—two great reasons which are really but one great reason—why I believe in God. I believe in God, my friends, I believe in God with all my soul, because this world is inexplicable without Him and explicable with Him, and because Jesus Christ believed in Him; and it was Jesus Christ that showed me that this world demanded God and was inexplicable without Him; that made certain every suspicion and dream that I had had before, and Jesus Christ believed in Him. Shall I go to the expert about chemistry or geology and ask him the truth with regard to the structure of the world and the meeting of its atoms and forces? And shall not I go to the spiritual expert, to him in whom the spiritual life of man has been clearest, and say, "O Christ, tell me what is the centre and source and end of all?" When he says, "God," shall I not believe Him?

It is impossible, as I have suggested to you again and again in what I have been saying, that a man can have his mind open to the receipt of the truth of a person unless he be a certain kind of man himself. I do not know but the basest and the wickedest man who lives may believe in the Copernican theory, or that two and two make four, yet I cannot help believing that if he were a better and truer man he would believe even those truths, outside of himself, of science and arithmetic, more fully and deeply. Men were not all astray in the first thing that they were seeking after, though they were wofully astray in many things that they said about it, when they talked about faith and works. Faith enters in through the soul that does a noble deed, and in the coming in of that faith the higher deed becomes possible to him. Hear the words that Jesus said, words that our age must take to itself until it shall be wiser than it is to-day: "Blessed are the pure in heart, for they shall see God." "If any man will do His will, he shall know of the doctrine, whether it be of God." Ponder those words, my friends. See how reasonable they are. See how important they are. See how they have the secret of your own life, of what it is to do, of what it is to be, forever and ever sealed up in them. These two things, I am sure, are true with regard to the method of belief—that no man can ever go forward to a higher belief until he is true to the faith which he already holds. Be the noblest man that your present faith, poor and weak and imperfect as it is, can make you to be. Live up to your present growth, your present faith. So, and so only, as you take the next straight step forward, as you stand strong where you are now, so only can you think the curtain will draw back and there will be revealed to you what lies beyond. And then live in your positives and not in your negatives. I am tired of asking man what his religious faith is and having him tell me what he don't believe. He tells me that he don't believe in baptism or inspiration or in the trinity. If I asked a man where he was going and he told me he was not going to Washington, what could I know about where he was going? He would not go anywhere so long as he simply rested in that mere negative. Be done with saying what you don't believe, and find somewhere or other the truest, divinest thing to your soul that you do believe to-day, and work that out: work it out in all the action and consecration of the soul in the doing of your work. This I take to be the real freedom of Christian thought—when the man goes forward always into a fuller and fuller belief as he becomes obedient to that which he already holds.

But yet I know I have not touched the opinion, the feeling, nay, I will say the black prejudice that is upon many, many minds. "Ah, but you have bound yourself," you say. "You have given your assent to a certain creed, you believe certain dogmas. To put it as simply as you have put it to us this morning, you believe a certain person. I, I am free, I believe nothing, I can go wandering here and everywhere and disbelieve to my heart's content." Yes, I do believe something, and I thank God for it. But I deny with all my intelligence and soul the very idea that in believing that something I have shut my soul to evidence. I am ready to hear any man living, any man living to-day who will prove to me that the Christ has never lived and that he is not the Lord of men. I will listen to any man who is in earnest and who is sincere. I will not listen to any trifler, caviller, who is merely trying to make a point and to get ahead of the poor arguments that I can use; but let any fellow-man come to me with an earnest face, either of puzzled doubt, or of earnest and convinced unbelief, and say to me, "Are you not wrong?" or "I believe that you are wrong," and I, of course, will talk to him. Do I want to believe anything that cannot be proved to be true, anything that my intelligence shall not receive? Why should I believe it? Shall I trust myself to the ship merely because I have refused to examine its timbers, when men tell me that it is unsound? Shall I throw away my truthfulness simply for the sake of holding what I want, what I choose to call the truth? It is not because it is safe, it is not because it is pleasant, it is because it seems to the Christian man to be true, that the Christian man believes in the presence, the life, the power of Jesus Christ. Therefore come, let me hear every one of you what you have to say. Let me see where that upon which my soul rests for its very life breaks down; but, until I hear, I will go forward, strong in the assurance of that which takes hold of all my life, convinces my reason, lays hold of my affections, enlarges my actions, and opens my whole being to the freedom of the child of God.

And why should not you, my friends, why should not you? I honor the sceptic, the faithful and devout sceptic, with all my soul. I am no scorner of the man who, without scorn, finds it impossible to accept that which to my soul seems to be the absolute truth. I will scorn only that which God scorns. He scorns the scorner, and only the scorning man is worthy of the scorn of human kind. But while I honor the sceptic, while I invite him to make manifest his scepticism, not merely for his sake but for my own, I will not hold, I cannot hold that he is living a larger life than the man whom the Christ invites to every noble duty, to every faithful fulfilment of himself. I will feel that he, perhaps by the necessity of his nature, perhaps by his circumstances, perhaps by something which came down to him from his ancestors, is shut in, is a contained and hampered and hindered man, and I will long for the day when he, lifting up his eyes, sees that Christ walking in the midst of humanity, and yet at the head of humanity, manifesting our human nature, but outgoing our human nature, glorifying our streets while He interprets our streets for the first time into their full meaning, giving to our shops and houses a radiancy which they have expected and dreamed of, but never felt, and tempting us always into a deeper belief in Him, which, embodying itself in a completer consecration to the right and true, shall lead us on into the fulness which he fills. Can I, can you, have Christ in human history, Christ in the world, and live as if He were not here? Will you not give yourself to that of Him which you know to-day? Will you not at least lay hold of the very skirts of His garment and say, "I see that Thou art good, I see that Thou art true. Lead me into the goodness and truth which by communion and sympathy shall know Thee more. Lord, I believe. I believe just a little. Lord, I know that that must come which Thou hast said has come in Thee. I would enter into Thee, to see whether it has indeed come in Thee, and Thou shalt lead me, Thou shalt teach me. Lord, I believe. I have not grasped Thee. No man has grasped Thee. The man who says that he has grasped Thee proves thereby that he does not know Thee. I know that I have not grasped Thee, but I will follow Thee by doing righteousness, by serving truth, by knowing and acknowledging Thee until all of that shall become clear to me. I will follow Thee, and Thou shalt lead me into the glory which Thou Thyself abidest in. Lord, I believe, Lord, I believe, help Thou mine unbelief." The story of the present, the hope, the pure, certain hope of the future is in those great words: "Lord, I believe, help Thou mine unbelief."

# III. THE DUTY OF THE CHRISTIAN BUSINESS MAN.

I will read to you once again the words which I have read before,
the words of Jesus in the eighth chapter of the Gospel of St. John:

> "As He spake these words, many believed on
> Him. Then said Jesus to those Jews which believed
> on Him, if ye continue in My word, then are ye My
> disciples indeed; and ye shall know the truth, and
> the truth shall make you free. They answered Him,
> We be Abraham's seed, and were never in bondage
> to any man: how sayest Thou, Ye shall be made
> free? Jesus answered them, Verily, verily, I say un-
> to you. Whosoever committeth sin is the servant of
> sin. And the servant abideth not in the house for-
> ever: but the Son abideth ever. If the Son therefore
> shall make you free, ye shall be free indeed."

I do not know how any man can stand and plead with his brethren for the higher life, that they will enter into and make their own
the life of Christ and God, unless he is perpetually conscious that
around them with whom he pleads there is the perpetual pleading
and the voice of God Himself. Unless a man believes that, everything that he has to say must seem, in the first place, impertinent,
and, in the second place, almost absolutely hopeless. Who is man
that he shall plead with his fellow-man for the change of a life, for
the entrance into a whole new career, for the alteration of a spirit,
for the surrounding of himself with a new region in which he has
not lived before? But if it be so, that God is pleading with every one
of His children to enter into the highest life; if it be so, that God is
making His application and His appeal to every soul to know Him,
and in Him to know himself, then one may plead with earnestness
and plead with great hopefulness before his brethren. And so it is.
The great truth of Jesus Christ is that, that God is pleading with
every soul, not merely in the words which we hear from one anoth-

er, not merely in the words which we read from His book, but in every influence of life; and, in those unknown influences which are too subtle for us to understand or perceive, God is forever seeking after the souls of His children.

I cannot stand before you for the last time that I shall stand In these meetings, my friends, without reminding myself and without reminding you of that; without reminding myself also and without trying to remind you of how absolutely conformable it is to everything that man does in this world. The great richness of nature, the great richness of life, comes when we understand that behind every specific action of man there is some one of the more elemental and primary forces of the universe that are always trying to express themselves. There is nothing that man does that finds its beginning within itself, but everything, every work of every trade, of every occupation, is simply the utterance of some one of those great forces which lie behind all life, and in the various ways of the different generations and of the different men are always trying to make their mark upon the world. Behind the power that the man exercises there always lies the great power of life, the continual struggle of nature to write herself in the life and work of man, the power of beauty struggling to manifest itself, the harmony that is always desiring to make itself known. To the merchant there are the great laws of trade, of which his works are but the immediate expression. To the mechanic there are the continual forces of nature, gravitation uttering itself in all its majesty, made no less majestic because it simply takes its expression for the moment in some particular exercise of his art. To the ship that sails upon the sea there are the everlasting winds that come out of the treasuries of God and fulfil His purpose in carrying His children to their destination. There is no perfection of the universe and of the special life of man in the universe until it comes to this. The greatest of all forces are ready without condescension, are ready as the true expression of their life, to manifest themselves in the particular activities which we find everywhere, and which are going on everywhere. The little child digs his well in the sea-shore sand, and the great Atlantic, miles deep, miles wide, is stirred all through and through to fill it for him. Shall it not be so then here to-day, and shall it not be the truth, upon which we let our minds especially dwell, and which we keep in our souls all the time that I am speaking and you are listening, that however He may be hidden from our sight God is the ultimate fact and the final purpose and power of the universe, and that everything that man tries to do for his fellow-man is but the expression of that love of God which is everywhere struggling to utter itself in blessing, to give itself away to the soul of every one for whom He cares?

It is in this truth that I find the real secret, the deepest meaning, of the everlasting dissatisfaction of man that is always ready to be stirred. We moralize, we philosophize about the discontent of man. We give little reasons for it; but the real reason of it all is this, that which everything lying behind it really signifies: that man is greater than his circumstances, and that God is always calling to him to come up to the fulness of his life. Dreadful will be the day when the world becomes contented, when one great universal satisfaction spreads itself over the world. Sad will be the day for every man when he becomes absolutely contented with the life that he is living, with the thoughts that he is thinking, with the deeds that he is doing, when there is not forever beating at the doors of his soul some great desire to do something larger, which he knows that he was meant and made to do because he is the child of God. And there is the real secret of the man's struggle with his sins. It is not simply the hatefulness of the sin, as we have said again and again, but it is the dim perception, the deep suspicion, the real knowledge at the heart of the man, that there is a richer and a sinless region in which it is really meant for him to dwell. Man stands separated from that life of God, as it were, by a great, thick wall, and every effort to put away his sin, to make himself a nobler and a purer man, is simply his beating at the inside of that door which stands between him and the life of God, which he knows that he ought to be living. It is like the prisoner hidden in his cave, who feels through all the thick wall that shuts him out from it the sunlight and the joyous life that is outside, who knows that his imprisonment is not his true condition, and so with every tool that his hands can grasp and with his bleeding hands themselves beats on the stone, that he may find his way out. And the glory and the beauty of it is that while he is beating upon the inside of the wall there is also a noble power praying upon the outside of that wall, The life to which he ought to come is striving in its turn, upon its side, to break away the hindrance that is keeping him from the thing he ought to be, that is keeping him from the life he ought to live. God, with His sunshine and lightning, with the great majestic manifestations of Himself, and with all the peaceful exhibitions of His life, is forever trying, upon His side of the wall, to break away the great barrier that separates the sinner's life from Him. Great is the power, great is the courage of the sinner, when through the thickness of the walls he feels that beating life of God, when he knows that he is not working alone, when he is sure that God is wanting him just as truly, far more truly, than he wants God. He bears himself to a nobler struggle with his enemy and a more determined effort to break down the resistance that stands between him and the higher life. Our figure is all imperfect, as all our figures are so imperfect, because it seems to be the man all by himself, working by himself, until he shall come forth into the life of God, as if God waited there to receive him when he came forth the freed man, and as if the working of the freedom upon the sinner's side had not something also of the purpose of God within him. God is not merely in the sunshine; God is in the cavern of the man's sin. God is with the sinner wherever he can be. There is no soul so black in its sinfulness, so determined in its defiant obstinacy, that God has abandoned his throne room at the centre of the sinner's life, and every movement is the God movement and every effort is the God force, with which man tries to break forth from his sin and come forth into the full sunlight of a life with God. Do you not think how full of hope it is? Do you not see that when this great conception of the universe, which is Christ's conception, which beamed in every look that He shed upon the world, which was told in every word that He spoke and which was in every movement of His hand—do you not see how, when this great conception of the universe takes possession of a man, then all his struggle with his sin is changed, it becomes a strong struggle, a glorious struggle. He hears perpetually the voice of Christ, "Be of good cheer. I have overcome the world. You shall overcome it by the same strength which overcame with Me."

And then another thing. When a man comes forth into the fulness of that life with God, when at last he has entered God's service and the obedience to God's will, and the communion with God's life, then there comes this wonderful thing, there comes the revelation of the man's past. We dare to tell the man that if he enters into the divine life, if he makes himself a servant of God and does God's will out of obedient love, he shall then be strong and wise. One great element of his strength is going to be this: A marvellous revelation that is to come to him of how all his past has been filled with the power of that spirit with which he has at last entered into communion, to which he has at last submitted himself. Man becomes the child of God, becomes the servant of Jesus Christ, and this marvellous revelation amazes him. He sees that back through all the years of his most obstinate and careless life, through all his wilfulness and resistance, through all his profligacy and black sin, God has been with him all the time, beating himself upon his life, showing him how He desired to call him to Himself, and that the final submission does not win God. It simply submits to the God who has been with the soul all the time. Can there be anything more winning to the soul than that, anything that brings a deeper shame to you, than to have it revealed to you, suddenly or slowly, that from the first day that you came into this world, nay, before your life was an uttered fact in this world, God has been loving you, and seeking you, and planning for you, and making every effort that He could make in consistency with the free will with which He endowed you from the centre of His own life, that you might become His and therefore might become truly yourself? Through all the years in which you were obstinate and rebellious, through all the years in which you defied Him, nay, through the years in which you denied Him and said that He did not exist, He was with you all the time. What shall I say to my friend who is an atheist? Shall I believe that until he comes to a change of his opinions and recognizes that there is indeed a ruling love, a great and fatherly God for all the world, that he has nothing to do with that God? Shall I believe that God has nothing to do with him until he acknowledges God? God would be no God to me if He were that, if He left the man absolutely unhelped until the man beat at the doors of His divine helpfulness and said, "I believe in Thee at last. Now help me." And to the atheist there appears the light of the God whom he denies. Into every soul, just so far and just so fast as it is possible for that soul to receive it, God beats His life and gives His help. That is what makes a man hopeful of all his fellow-men as he looks around upon them and sees them in all the conditions of their life.

And this could only be if that were true, if that is true, which we are dwelling upon constantly, the absolute naturalness of the Christian life, that it is man's true life, that it is no foreign region into which some man may be transported and where he lives an alien to all his own essential nature and to all the natural habitudes in which he is intending to exist. There are two ideas of religion which always have abounded, and our great hope is, our great assurance for the future of the world is, that the true and pure idea of religion some day shall grow and take possession of the life of man. One idea, held by very earnest people, embodied in very faithful and devoted lives, is the strangeness of religion to the life of man, as if some morning something dropped out of the sky that had had no place upon our earth before, as if there came the summons to man to be something entirely different from what the conditions of his nature prophesied and intended that he should be. The other idea is that religion comet by the utterance of God from the heavens, but comes up out of the human life of man; that man is essentially and intrinsically religious; that he does not become something else than man when he becomes the servant of Jesus Christ, but then for the first time he becomes man; that religion is not something that is fastened upon the outside of his life, but is the awakening of the truth inside of his life; the Church is but the true fulfilment of human life and society; heaven is but the New Jerusalem that completes all the old Jerusalem and Londons and Bostons that have been here upon our earth. Man, in the fulfilment of his nature by Jesus Christ, is man—not to be something else, our whole humanity is too dear to us. I will cling to this humanity of man, for I do love it, and I will know nothing else. But when man is bidden to look back into his humanity and see what it means to be a man, that humanity means purity, truthfulness, earnestness, and faithfulness to that God of which humanity is a part, that God which manifested that humanity was a part of it, when the incarnation showed how close the divine and human belonged together—when man hears that voice, I do not know how he can resist, why he shall not lift himself up and say, "Now I can be a man, and I can be man only as I share in and give my obedience to and enter into communion with the life of

God," and say to Christ, to Christ the revealer of all this, "Here I am, fulfil my manhood."

And do not you see how immediately this sweeps aside, as one gush of the sunlight sweeps aside the darkness, do not you see how it sweeps aside all the foolish and little things that people are saying? I say to my friend, "Be a Christian." That means to be a full man. And he says to me, "I have not time to be a Christian. I have not room. If my life was not so full. You don't know how hard I work from morning to night. What time is there for me to be a Christian? What time is there, what room is there for Christianity in such a life as mine?" But does not it come to seem to us so strange, so absurd, if it was not so melancholy, that man should say such a thing as that? It is as if the engine had said it had no room for the steam. It is as if the tree had said it had no room for the sap. It is as if the ocean had said it had no room for the tide. It is as if the man said that he had no room for his soul. It is as if life said that it had no time to live, when it is life. It is not something that is added to life. It is life. A man is not living without it. And for a man to say that "I am so full in life that I have no room for life," you see immediately to what absurdity it reduces itself. And how a man knows what he is called upon by God's voice, speaking to him every hour, speaking to him every moment, speaking to him out of everything, that which the man is called upon to do because it is the man's only life! Therefore time, room, that is what time, that is what room is for—life. Life is the thing we seek, and man finds it in the fulfilment of his life by Jesus Christ.

Now, until we understand this and take it in its richness, all religion seems, becomes to us such a little thing that it is not religion at all. You have got to know that religion, the service of Christ, is not something to be taken in in addition to your life; it is your life. It is not a ribbon that you shall tie in your hat, and go down the street declaring yourself that you have accepted something in addition to the life which your fellow-men are living. It is something which, taken into your heart, shall glow in every action so that your fellow-men shall say, "Lo, how he lives! What new life has come into him?" It is that insistence upon the great essentialness of the religious life, it is the insistence that religion is not a lot of things that a man does, but is a new life that a man lives, uttering itself in new actions because it is the new life. "Except a man be born again he cannot see the kingdom of God." So Jesus said to Nicodemus the ruler, Nicodemus the amateur in religions, who came and said, "Perhaps this teacher has something else that I can bind into my catalogue of truths and hold it." Jesus looked him in the face and said: "It is not that, my friend, it is not that; it is to be a new man, it is to be born again. It is to have the new life, which is the old life, which is the eternal life. So alone does man enter into the kingdom of God." I cannot help believing all the time that if our young men knew this, religion would lift itself up and have a dignity and greatness—not a thing for weak souls, but a thing for the manliest soul. Just because of its manliness it is easy. "Is it easy or is it hard, this religion of yours?" people say to us. I am sure I do not know the easy and the hard things. I cannot tell the difference. What is easier than for a man to breathe? And yet, have you never seen a breathless man, a man in whom the breathing was almost stopped, a drowning man, an exhausted man? have you never seen, when the breath was put once more to his nostrils and brought down once more into his empty lungs, the struggle with which he came back to it? It was the hardest thing for him to do, so much harder for him to live than it was for him to die. But by and by see him on his feet, going about his work, helping his fellow-men, living his life, rejoicing in his days, guarding against his dangers, full of life. Is life a hard thing for him? You don't talk about its being hard or easy any more than you talk about life itself. The man who lives in God knows no life except the life of God. Let men know that it is not mere trifling, it is not a thing to be dallied with for an instant, it is not a thing for a man to convince himself by an argument, and then keep as it were locked in a shelf: it is something that is so deep and serious, so deep and serious that when a man has once tested it there is no more chance of his going out of it than there is of his going out of the friendship and the love which holds him with its perpetual expression, with the continued deeper and deeper manifestation of the way in which the living being belongs to him who has a right to his life.

Now in the few moments that remain I want to take it for granted most seriously, most earnestly, that the men who are listening to me are in earnest, and I want to try to tell them as a brother might tell a brother, as I might tell to you or try to tell to you if sitting before my fireside, I want to try to answer the question which I know is upon your hearts. "What shall I do about this?" I know you say; "Is this all in the clouds? Is there anything I can do in the right way?" If you are in earnest, I shall try to tell you what I should do, if I were in your place, that I might enter into that life and be the free man that we have tried to describe, of whom we believe certain special and definite things. What are they? In the first place I would put away my sin. There is not a man listening to me now who has not some trick of life, some habit that has possession of him, which he knows is a wrong thing. The very first thing for a man to do is absolutely to set himself against them. If you are foul, stop being licentious, at least stop doing licentious things. If you, in any part of your business, are tricky, and unsound, and unjust, cut that off, no matter what it costs you. There is something clear and definite enough for every man. It is as clear for every man as the sunlight that smites him in his eyes. Stop doing the bad thing which you are doing. It is drawing the bolt away to let whatever mercy may come in come in. Stop doing your sin. You can do that if you will. Stop doing your sin, no matter how mechanical it seems, and then take up your duty, whatever you can do to make the world more bright and good. Do whatever you can to help every struggling soul, to add new strength to any staggering cause, the poor sick man that is by you, the poor wronged man whom you with your influence might vindicate, the poor boy in your shop that you may set with new hope upon the road of life that is beginning already to look dark to him. I cannot tell you what it is. But you know your duty. No man ever looked for it and did not find it.

And then the third thing—pray. Yes, go to the God whom you but dimly see and pray to Him in the darkness, where He seems to sit. Ask Him, as if He were, that He will give you that which, if He is, must come from Him, can come from Him alone. Pray anxiously. Pray passionately, in the simplest of all words, with the simplest of all thoughts. Pray, the manliest thing that a man can do, the fastening of his life to the eternal, the drinking of his thirsty soul out of the great fountain of life. And pray distinctly. Pray upon your knees. One grows tired sometimes of the free thought, which is yet perfectly true, that a man can pray anywhere and anyhow. But men have found it good to make the whole system pray. Kneel down, and the very bending of these obstinate and unused knees of yours will make the soul kneel down in the humility in which it can be exalted in the sight of God.

And then read your Bible. How cold that sounds! What, read a book to save my soul? Read an old story that my life in these new days shall be regenerated and saved? Yes, do just that, for out of that book, if you read it truly, shall come the divine and human person. If you can read it with your soul as well as with your eyes, there shall come the Christ there walking in Palestine. You shall see Him so much greater than the Palestine in which he walks, that at one word of prayer, as you bend over the illuminated page, there shall lift up that body-being of the Christ, and come down through the centuries and be your helper at your side. So read your Bible.

And then seek the Church—oh, yes, the Church. Do you think, my friends, you who stand outside the Church, and blame her for her inconsistencies, and tell of her shortcomings, and point out the corruptions that are in her history, all that are in her present life to-day—do you really believe that there is an earnest man in the Church that does not know the Church's weaknesses and faults just as well as you do? Do you believe that there is one of us living in the life and heart of the Church who don't think with all his conscience, who don't in every day in deep distress and sorrow know how the Church fails of the great life of the Master, how far she is from being what God meant she should be, what she shall be some day? But all the more I will put my life into that Church, all the more I will drink the strength that she can give to me and make what humble contribution to her I can bring of the earnestness and faithfulness of my life. Come into the Church of Jesus Christ. There is no other body on the face of the earth that represents what she represents—the noble destiny of the human soul, the great capacity of human faith, the inexhaustible and unutterable love of God, the Christ, who stands to manifest them all.

Now those are the things for a man to do who really cares about all this. Those are the things for an earnest man to do. They have no power in themselves, but they are the opening of the windows. And if that which I believe is true, God is everywhere giving himself to us, the opening of the windows is a signal that we want Him and an invitation that He will be glad enough to answer, to come. Into every window that is open to Him and turned His way, Christ comes, God comes. That is the only story. There is put aside everything else. Election, predestination, they can go where they please. I am sure that God gives Himself to every soul that wants Him and declares its want by the open readiness of the signal which He knows. How did the sun rise on our city this morning? Starting up in the east, the sun came in its majesty into the sky. It smote on the eastward windows, and wherever the window was all closed, even if it were turned eastward, on the sacred side of the city's life, it could not come in; but wherever any eastward window had its curtains drawn, wherever he who slept had left the blinds shut, so that the sun when it came might find its way into his sleepiness, there the sun came, and with a shout awoke its faithful servant who had believed in him even before he had seen him, and said, "Arise, arise from the dead, and I will give thee life." This is the simplicity of it all, my friends. A multitude of other things you need not trouble yourselves about. I amaze myself when I think how men go asking about the questions of eternal punishment and the duration of man's torment in another life, of what will happen to any man who does not obey Jesus Christ. Oh, my friends, the soul is all wrong when it asks that. Not until the soul says, "What will come if I do obey Jesus Christ?" and opens its glorified vision to see all the great things that are given to the soul that enters into the service of the perfect one, the perfect love, not until then the perfect love, the perfect life, come in. A man may be—I believe it with all my heart—so absolutely wrapped up in the glory of obedience, and the higher life, and the service of Christ, that he never once asks himself, "What will come to me if I do not obey?" any more than your child asks you what you will do to him if he is not obedient. Every impulse and desire of his life sets toward obedience. And so the soul may have no theory of everlasting or of limited punishment, or of the other life.

Simply now, here, he must have that without which he cannot live, that without which there is no life. Jesus the soul must have, the one yesterday, to-day, and forever; He that is and was and is to be. Men dwell upon what He was, upon what He is; I rather think to-day of what He is to be. And when I see these young men here before me looking to the future and not to the past, — nay, looking to the future and not to the present, valuing the present only as it is the seed ground of the future, the foundation upon which the structure is to rise whose pinnacle shall some day pierce the sky, — I want to tell them of the Jesus that shall be. In fuller comprehension of Him, with deeper understanding of His life, with a more entire impression of what He is and of what He may be to the soul, so men shall understand Him in the days to be, and yet He shall be the same Christ still. The future belongs to Jesus Christ, yes, the same Christ that I believe in and that I call upon you to believe in to-day, but a larger, fuller, more completely comprehended Christ, the Christ that is to be, the same Christ that was and suffered, the same Christ that is and helps, but the same Christ also who, being forever deeper and deeper and more deeply received into the souls of men, regenerates their institutions, changes their life, opens their capacities, surprises them with themselves, makes the world glorious and joyous every day, because it has become the new incarnation, the new presence of the divine life in the life of man.

Men are talking about the institutions in which you are engaged, my friends, about the business from which you have come here to worship for this little hour. Men are questioning about what they care to do, what they can have to do with Christianity. They are asking everywhere this question: "Is it possible for a man to be engaged in the activities of our modern life and yet to be a Christian? Is it possible for a man to be a broker, a shopkeeper, a lawyer, a mechanic, is it possible for a man to be engaged in a business of to-day, and yet love his God and his fellow-man as himself?" I do not know. I do not know what transformations these dear businesses of yours have got to undergo before they shall be true and ideal homes for the child of God; but I do know that upon Christian merchants and Christian brokers and Christian lawyers and Christian men in business to-day there rests an awful and a beautiful responsibility: to prove, if you can prove it, that these things are capable of being made divine, to prove that a man can do the work that you have been doing this morning and will do this afternoon, and yet shall love his God and his fellow-man as himself. If he cannot, if he cannot, what business have you to be doing them? If he can, what business have you to be doing them so poorly, so carnally, so unspiritually, that men look on them and shake their heads with doubt? It belongs to Christ in men first to prove that man may be a Christian and yet do business; and, in the second place, to show how a man, as he becomes a greater Christian, shall purify and lift the business that he does and make it the worthy occupation of the Son of God.

What shall be our universal law of life? Can we give it as we draw toward our last moment? I think we can. I want to live, I want to live, if God will give me help, such a life that, if all men in the world were living it, this world would be regenerated and saved. I want to live such a life that, if that life changed into new personal peculiarities as it went to different men, but the same life still, if every man were living it, the millennium would be here; nay, heaven would be here, the universal presence of God. Are you living that life now? Do you want your life multiplied by the thousand million so that all men shall be like you, or don't you shudder at the thought, don't you give hope that other men are better than you are? Keep that fear, but only that it may be the food of a diviner hope, that all the world may see in you the thing that man was meant to be, that is, the Christ. Ah, you say, that great world, it is too big; how can I stretch my thought and imagination and conscience to the poor creatures in Africa and everywhere? Then bring it home. Ah, this dear city of ours, this city that we love, this city in which many of us were born, in which all of us are finding the rich and sweet associations of our life, this city, whose very streets we love because they come so close to everything we do and are, cannot we do something for it? Cannot we make its life diviner? Cannot we contribute something that it has not to-day? Cannot you put in it, some little corner of it, a life which others shall see and say, "Ah, that our lives may be like that!" And then the good Boston in which we so rejoice, which we so love, which we would so fain make a part of the kingdom of God, a true city of Jesus Christ, we shall not die without having done something for it.

I linger, and yet I must not linger. Oh, my friends, oh, my fellowmen, it is not very long that we shall be here. It is not very long. This life for which we are so careful—it is not very long; and yet it is so long, because, long, long after we have passed away out of men's sight and out of men's memory, the world, with something that we have left upon it, that we have left within it, will be going on still. It is so long because, long after the city and the world have passed away, we shall go on somewhere, somehow, the same beings still, carrying into the depths of eternity something that this world has done for us that no other world could do, something of goodness to get now that will be of value to us a million years hence, that we never could get unless we got it in the short years of this earthly life. Will you know it? Will you let Christ teach it to you? Will you let Christ tell you what is the perfect man? Will you let Him set His simplicity and graciousness close to your life, and will you feel their power? Oh! be brave, be true, be pure, be men, be men in the power of Jesus Christ. May God bless you! May God bless you! Let us pray.

# IV. TRUE LIBERTY.

An earnest appeal to all that enter that Liberty. May I read to you a few words from the eighth chapter of St. John? "Then said Jesus to those Jews which believed on Him, If ye continue in my word, then are ye my disciples indeed; and ye shall know the truth, and the truth shall make you free."

Let us not think, my friends, that there is anything strange about the spectacle which we witnessed this morning. The only strange thing that there could be about it is that anybody should think that it is strange that men should turn aside for half an hour from their ordinary business pursuits, that they should come from the details of life to inquire in regard to the principles, the everlasting principles and purposes of life; that they should turn aside from those things which are occupying them from day to day and make one single hour in the week consecrated to the service of those great things which underlie all life—surely there is nothing very strange. There is nothing more absolutely natural. Every man does it in his own sort of way, in his own choice of time. We have chosen to do it together, on one day of the week during these few weeks which the Christian Church has so largely set apart for special thought and prayer and earnest attempt to approach the God to whom we belong. It is simply as if the stream turned back again to its fountain, that it might refresh itself and make itself strong for the great work that it had to do in watering the fields and turning the wheels of industry. It is simply as if men plodding along over the flat routine of their life chose once in a while to go up into the mountain top, whence they might once in a while look abroad over their life, and understand more fully the way in which they ought to work. These are the principles, these are the pictures which represent that which we have in mind as we come together for a little while each Monday in these few weeks, in order that we may think about things of God and try to realize the depth of our own human life. The first thing that we ought to understand about it is that when we turn aside from life it is only that we go deeper into life. This hour does not stand apart from the rest of the hours of the week, in that we are dealing with things in which the rest of the week has no concern. He who understands life deeply and fully, understands life truly; he has forever renewed his life; and if there comes into our hearts, in the life which we are living, a perpetual sense that life needs renewal, a richening and refreshing, then it is in order that we may go down into the depths and see what lies at the root of things—things that we are perpetually doing and thinking. It is this that brought us together here: it is that we may open to ourselves some newer, higher life. It is that we may understand the life that we may live, along side of and as a richer development of that life which we are living from day to day, which we have been living during the years of our life. How that idea has haunted men in every period of their existence, how it is haunting you, that there is some higher life which it is possible to live! There has never been a religion that has not started there, lifted up its eyes and seen, afar off, what it was possible for man to do from day to day, in contrast with the things which men immediately and presently are. There is not any moment of the human soul which has not rested upon some great conception that man was a nobler being than he was ordinarily conceiving himself to be; that he was not destined to the things which were ordinarily occupying his life; that he might be living a greater and nobler life. It is because the Christian Scriptures have laid most earnestly hold of this idea, it is because it was represented not simply in the words which Christ said, but in the very being which Christ was, that we go to them to get the inspiration and the indication, the revelation and the enlightenment which we need. I have read to you these few words in which Christ declares the whole subject, the whole character of which His life is and what His work is about to do, because it seems to me that they strike at once the key-note of that which we want to understand. They let us enter into the full conception of that which the new life which is offered to man really is. There are two conceptions which come to every man when he is entering upon a new life, changing his present life to something that is different from the present life, and being a different sort of creature and living in a different sort of a way. The first way in which it presents itself to him—almost always at the beginning of every religion, perhaps—is in the way of restraint and imprisonment. Man thinks of every change that is to come to him as in the nature of denial of something that he is at the present doing and being, as the laying hold upon himself of some sort of restraint, bringing to him something which says: "I must not do the thing which I am doing. I must lay upon myself restraints, restrictions, commandments, and prohibitions. I must not let myself be the man that I am." You see how the Old Testament comes before the New Testament, the law ringing from the mountain top with the great denials, the great prohibitions, that come from the mouth of God. "Thou shalt not do this, that, or the other—Thou shalt not murder. Thou shalt not steal. Thou shalt not commit adultery. Thou shalt not covet thy neighbor's goods." That is the first conception which comes to a man of the way in which he is to enter upon a new life, of the way in which the denial in his experience is to take effect. It is as if the hands were stretched out in order that fetters might be placed upon them. The man says, "Let some power come that is to hinder me from being this thing that I am." And the whole notion is the notion of imprisonment, restraint So it is with all civilization. It is perfectly possible for us to represent civilization as compared with barbarism, as accepted by mankind, as a great mass of restrictions and prohibitions that have been laid upon human life, so that the freedom of life has been cast aside, and man has entered into restricted, restrained, and imprisoned condition. So it is with every fulfilment of life. It is possible for a man always to represent it to himself as if it were the restriction, restraint, and prohibition of his life. The man passes onward into the fuller life which belongs to a man. He merges his selfishness into that richer life which is offered to human kind. He makes himself, instead of a single, selfish man, a man of family; and it is easy enough to consider that marriage and the family life bring immediately restraints and prohibitions. The man may not have the freedom which he used to have. So all development of education, in the first place, offers itself to man, or seems to offer itself to man, as prohibition and imprisonment and restraint. There is no doubt truth in such an idea. We never lose sight of it. No other richer and fuller idea which we come to by and by ever does away with the thought that man's advance means prohibition and self-denial, that in order that man shall become the greater thing he must cease to be the poorer and smaller thing he has been. But yet there is immediately a greater and fuller. When we hear those words of Jesus, we see immediately that not the idea of imprisonment but the idea of liberty, not the idea of restraint but that of setting free, is the idea which is really in His mind when he offers the fullest life to human kind. Have you often thought of how the whole Bible is a Book of Liberty, of how It rings with liberty from beginning to end, of how the great men are the men of liberty, of how the Old Testament, the great picture which forever shines, is the emancipator, leading forth out of imprisonment the people of God, who were to do the great work of God in the very much larger and freer life in which they were to live? The prophet, the psalmist, are ever preaching and singing about liberty, the enfranchisement of the life of man, that man was not imprisoned in order to fulfil himself, but shall open his life, and every new progress shall be into a new region of existence which lie has not touched as yet. When we turn from the Old Testament to the New Testament, how absolutely clear that idea is! Christ is the very embodiment of human liberty. In His own personal life and in everything that He did and said, He was forever uttering the great gospel that man, in order to become his completest, must become his freest, that what a man did when he entered into a new life was to open a new region in which new powers were to find their exercise, in which he was to be able to be and do things which he could not be and do in more restricted life. It is the acceptance of that idea, it seems to me, that makes us true disciples of Christ and of that great gospel, and that transfigures everything. When my friend turns over some new leaf, as we say, and begins to live a new life, what shall we think of him? I learn that he has become a Christian man, that he is doing something, that he is working in a way and living a life which I have not known before. What is my impression in regard to him? Is not your impression, as you look upon that man, that somehow or other he has entered into a slavery or bondage, that he has taken upon his life restrictions and imprisonments which he did not have before? And you think of him, perhaps, as a man who has done a wise and prudent thing, who has done something that is going to be for his benefit some day in some distant and half-realized world, but as a man who, for the present, has laid a burden and bondage upon his life. That is never the tone of Christ; it is never the tone of the Christian gospel. When a man turns away from his sins and enters into energetic holiness, when a man sacrifices his own self-indulgence and goes forth a pure servant of his God and his fellow-men, there is only one cry in the whole gospel of that man, and that is the cry of freedom. As soon as he can catch that, as soon as I can feel about my friend, who has become a better man, that he has become a larger and not a smaller, a freer and not a more imprisoned man, as soon as I lift up my voice and say that the man is free, then I understand him more fully, and he becomes a revelation to me in the higher and richer life which is possible for me to live. But think of it for yourselves, for a moment, and ask what freer life really is. Try to give a definition of liberty, and I know not what it can be said to be except something of this kind: Liberty is the fullest opportunity for man to be and do the very best that is possible for him. I know of no definition of liberty, that oldest and dearest phrase of men, and sometimes the vaguest also, except that. It has been perverted, it has been distorted and mystified, but that is what it really means: the fullest opportunity for a man to do and be the very best that is in his personal nature to do and to be. It immediately follows that everything which is necessary for the full realization of a man's life, even though it seems to have the character of restraint for a moment, is really a part of the process of his enfranchisement, is the bringing forth of him to a fuller liberty. You see a man coming forward and offering himself as one of the defenders of his country in his country's need. You see him standing at the door where men are being received as recruits into the army of the country. He wants liberty. He wants to be able to do that which he cannot do in his poor, personal isolation here at home. He wants the badge which will give him the right to go forth and meet the enemies of his country, and he enrolls himself among these men. He makes himself subject to obligations, duties, and drill. They are a part of his enfranchisement. They are really the breaking of the fetters upon his slavery, the sending him forth into freedom. He is like a bit of iron or steel that lies upon the ground. It lies neglected and perfectly free. You see it is made by the adjustment of the end of it so that it can be set into a great machine and become part of a great working system. But there it lies. Will you call it free? It is bound to be nothing there. It is absolutely separate, and with its own personality distinct and individual and all alone. What is to make that bit of iron a free bit of iron, to let it go forth and do the thing which it was meant to do, but the taking of it and the binding of it at both ends into the structure of which it was made to be a part? It seems to me the binding of a man,—it seems to me that the binding of the iron is not the yielding of its freedom. It is not merely after finding its place within the system that it first achieves its freedom and so joins in the music and partakes of the courses with which the whole enginery is filled. Is not it, then, for the first time a free bit of iron, having accomplished all that it was made to do when it came forth from the forge of the master, who had this purpose in his mind? This, then, is freedom; everything is part of the enfranchisement of a man which helps to put him in the place where he can live his best. Therefore every duty, every will of God, every commandment of Christ, every self-surrender that a man is called upon to obey or to make—do not think of it as if it were simply a restraint to liberty, but think of it as the very means of freedom, by which we realize the very purpose of God and the fulfilment of our life. It is interesting to see how all that is true in regard to the matter of belief, doctrine, and opinions which we are apt to accept. How strange it very often seems that men go to the Church, or to one another, and say: "Must I believe this doctrine in order that I can enter into the Church?" "Must I believe this doctrine in order that I may be saved?" men say, with a strange sort of notion about what salvation is. How strange it seems, when we really have got our intelligence about us and know what it is to believe! To believe a new truth, if it be really truth and we really believe it, is to have entered into a new region, in which our life shall find a new expansion and a new youth. Therefore, not "Must we believe?" but "May I believe?" is the true cry of the human creature who is seeking for the richest fulfilment of his life, who is working that his whole nature may find its complete expansion and so its completest exercise. We talk a great deal in these days and in this place about a liberal faith. What is a liberal faith, my friends? It seems to me that by every true meaning of the word, by every true thought of the idea, a liberal faith is a faith that believes much, and not a faith that believes little. The more a man believes, the more liberally he exercise his capacity of faith, the more he sends forth his intelligence into the mysteries of God, the more he understands those things which God chooses to reveal to his creatures, the more liberally he believes. Let yourselves never think that you grow liberal in faith by believing less; always be sure that the true liberality of faith can only come by believing more. It is true, indeed, that as soon as a man becomes eager for belief, for the truth of God and for the mysteries with which God's universe is filled, he becomes all the more critical and careful. He will hot any longer, if he were before, be simply greedy of things to believe, so that if any superstition comes offering itself to him he will not gather it in indiscriminately and believe it without evidence, without examination. He becomes all the more critical and careful, the more he becomes assured that belief, and not unbelief, is the true condition of his life. The truth that God has entered into this world in wondrous ways and filled its life with Jesus Christ, the truth that man has a soul and not simply a body, that he has a spiritual need, that God cares for him and he is to care for himself, that there is an immortal life, and that that which we call faith is but the opening of a gate, the pushing back of a veil,—shall a man believe those things as imprisonments of his nature, and shall it not make him larger? Shall it not be the indulgence of his life when he enters into the great certainties which so are offered to his belief, believing them in his own way? Let us always feel that to accept a new belief is no to build a wall beyond which we cannot pass, but is to open the door to a great fresh, free region, in which our souls are to live. And just so it is when we come to the moral things of life. The man puts aside some sinfulness. He breaks down the wall that has been shutting his soul out of its highest life. He has been a drunkard, and he becomes a sober man. He has been a cheat, and becomes a faithful man. He has been a liar, and becomes a truthful man. He has been a profligate, and he becomes a pure man. What has happened to that man? Shall he simply think of himself as one who has crushed this passion, shut down this part of his life? Shall he simply think of himself as one who has taken a course of self-denial? Nay. It is self-indulgence that a man has really entered upon. It is an indulgence of the deepest part of his own nature, not of his unreal nature. He has risen and shaken himself like a lion, so that the dust has fallen from his mane, and all the great range of that life which God gave him to live lies before him. This is the everlasting inspiration. This is the illumination. I don't wonder that men refuse to give up evil if it simply seems to them to be giving up the evil way, and no vision opens before them of the thing that they may be and do. I don't wonder that, if the negative, restricting, imprisoning conception of the new life is all that a man gets hold of, he lingers again and again in the old life. But just as soon as the great world opens before him then it is like a prisoner going out of the prison door. Is there no lingering? Does not the baser part of him cling to the old prison, to the ease and the provision for him, to the absence of anxiety and of energy? I think there can hardly be a prisoner who, with any leap of heart, goes out of the prison door, when his term is finished, and does not even look into that black horror where he has been living, cast some lingering, longing look behind. He comes to the exigencies, to the demands of life, to the necessity of making himself once more a true man among his fellow-men. But does he stop? He comes forth, and if there be the soul of a man in him still, he enters into the new life with enthusiasm, and finds the new powers springing in him to their work. And if it be so with every special duty, then with that great thing which you and I are called upon to do—the total acceptance by our nature of the will of God, the total acceptance by our nature of the mastery of Jesus Christ. Oh! how this world has perverted words and meanings, that the mastery of Jesus Christ should seem to be the imprisonment and not the enfranchisement of the soul! When I bring a flower out of the darkness and set it in the sun, and let the sunlight come streaming down upon it, and the flower knows the sunlight for which it was made and opens its fragrance and beauty; when I take a dark pebble and put it into the stream and let the silver water go coursing down over it and bringing forth the hidden color that was in the bit of stone, opening the nature that is in them, the flower and stone rejoice. I can almost hear them sing in the field and in the stream. What then? Shall not man bring his nature out into the fullest illumination, and surprise himself by the things that he might do? Oh! the littleness of the lives that we are living! Oh! the way in which we fail to comprehend, or when we do comprehend, deny to ourselves the bigness of that thing which it is to be a man, to be a child of God! Sometimes it dawns upon us that we can see it opening into the vision of these men and women in the New Testament. Sometimes there opens to us the picture of this thing that we might be, and then there are truly the trial moments of our life. Then we lift up ourselves and claim our liberty or, dastardly or cowardly, slink back into the sluggish imprisonment in which we have been living. How does all this affect that which we are continually conscious of, urging upon ourselves and upon one another? How does it affect the whole question of a man's sins? Oh! these sins, the things we know so well! As we sit here and stand here one entire hour, as we talk in this sort of way, everybody knows the weaknesses of his own nature, the sins of his own soul. Don't you know it? What shall we think about those sins? It seems to me, my friends, that all this great picture of the liberty into which Christ sets man, in the first place does one thing which we are longing to see done in the world. It takes away the glamour and the splendor from sin. It breaks that spell by which men think that the evil thing is the glorious thing. If the evil thing be that which Christ has told us that the evil thing is—which I have no time to tell you now—if every sin that you do is not simply a stain upon your soul, but is keeping you out from some great and splendid thing which you might do, then is there any sort of splendor and glory about sin? How about the sins that you did when you were young men? How can you look back upon those sins and think what your life might have been if it had been pure from the beginning, think what you might have been if from the very beginning you had caught sight of what it was to be a man? And then your boy comes along. What are the men in this town doing largely in many and many a house, but letting their boys believe that the sins of their early life are glorious things, except that those things which they did, the base and wretched things that they were doing when they were fifteen and twenty and twenty-five and thirty years old, are the true career of a human nature, are the true entrance into human life? The miserable talk about sowing wild oats, about getting through the necessary conditions of life before a man comes to solemnity! Shame upon any man who, having passed through the sinful conditions and habits and dispositions of his earlier life, has not carried out of them an absolute shame for them, that shall let him say to his boy, by word and by every utterance of his life within the house where he and the boy live together, "Refrain, for they are abominable things!" To get rid of the glamour of sin, to get rid of the idea that it is a glorious thing to be dissipated instead of being concentrated to duty, to get rid of the idea that to be drunken and to be lustful are true and noble expressions of our abounding human life, to get rid of any idea that sin is aught but imprisonment, is to make those who come after us, and to make ourselves in what of life is left for us, gloriously ambitious for the freedom of purity, for a full entrance into that life over which sin has no dominion. And yet, at

the same time, don't you see that while sin thus becomes contempt-
ible when we think about the great illustration of the will of God
and Jesus Christ, don't you see how also it puts on a new horror?
That which I thought I was doing in the halls of my imprisonment I
have really been doing within the possible world of God in which I
might have been free. The moment I see what life might have been
to me, then any sin becomes dreadful to me. Have you ever thought
of how the world has stood in glory and honor before the sinless
humanity of Jesus Christ? If any life could prove, if any argument
could show on investigation to-day that Jesus did one sin in all his
life, that the perfect liberty which was his perfect purity was not
absolutely perfect, do you realize what a horror would seem to fall
down from the heavens, what a constraint and burden would be
laid upon the lives of men, how the gates of men's possibilities
would seem to close in upon them? It is because there has been that
one life which, because absolutely pure from sin, was absolutely
free; it is because man may look up and see in that life the revelation
and possibility of his own; it is because that life, echoing the great
cry throughout the world that man everywhere is the son of God,
offers the same purity—and so the same freedom—to all mankind;
it is for that reason that a man rejoices to cling to, to believe in, however impure his life is, the perfect purity, the sinlessness of the life
of Jesus. When you sin, my friends, it is a man that sins, and a man
is a child of God; and for a child of God to sin is an awful thing, not
simply for the stain that he brings into the divine nature that is in
him, but for the life from which it shuts him out, for the liberty
which he abandons, for the inthrallment which it lays upon the soul.
There is one thing that people say very carelessly that always seems
to me to be a dreadful thing for a man to say. They say it when they
talk about their lives to one another, and think about their lives to
themselves, and by and by very often say it upon their death-bed
with the last gasp, as though their entrance into the eternal world
had brought them no deeper enlightenment. One wonders what is
the revelation that comes to them when they stand upon the borders
of the other side and are in the full life and eternity of God. The
thing men say is, "I have done the very best I can." It is an awful
thing for a man to say. The man never lived, save he who perfected
our humanity, who ever did the very best he could. You dishonor
your life, you not simply shut your eyes to certain facts, you not

simply say an infinitely absurd and foolish thing, but you dishonor your human life if you say that you have done in any day of your life or in all the days of your life put together, the very best that you could, or been the very best man that you could be. You! what are you? Again I say, The child of God, and this which you have been, what is it? Look over it, see how selfish it has been, see how material it has been, how it has lived in the depths when it might have lived on the heights, see how it has lived in the little narrow range of selfishness when it might have been as broad as all humanity, nay, when it might have been as the God of humanity. Don't dare to say that in any day of your life, or in all your life together, you have done the best that you could. The Pharisee said it when he went up into the temple, and all the world has looked on with mingled pity and scorn at the blindness of the man who stood there and paraded his faithfulness; while all the world has bent with a pity that was near to love, a pity that was full of sympathy because man recognized his condition and experience, for the poor creature grovelling upon the pavement, unwilling and unable even to look upon the altar, but who, standing afar off, said, "God be merciful to me a sinner!" Whatever else you say, don't say, "I have been the very best I could." That means that you have not merely lived in the rooms of your imprisonment, but that you have been satisfied to count them the only possible rooms of your life, and that the great halls of your liberty have never opened themselves before you. Shall not they open themselves somehow to us to-day, my friends? Shall we not turn away from this hour and go back into our business, into our offices, into the shops, into the crowded streets, bearing new thoughts of the lives that we might live, feeling the fetters on our hands and feet, feeling many things as fetters which we have thought of as the ornament and glory of our life, determined to be unsatisfied forever until these fetters shall be stricken off and we have entered into the full liberty which comes to those alone who are dedicated to the service of God, to the completion of their own nature, to the acceptance of the grace of Christ, and to the attainment of the eternal glory of the spiritual life, first here and then hereafter, never hereafter, it may be, except here and now, certainly here and now, as the immediate, pressing privilege and duty of our lives? So let us stand up on our feet and know ourselves in all the richness and in all the awfulness of our human life. Let us know ourselves children of God, and claim the liberty which God has given to every one of his children who will take it. God bless you and give some of you, help some of us, to claim, as we have never claimed before, that freedom with which the Son makes free!

# V. THE CHRIST IN WHOM CHRISTIANS BE-LIEVE.

I want to read to you again the words of Jesus in the eighth chapter of the Gospel of St. John: "Then said Jesus to those Jews which believed on Him, If ye continue in my word, then are ye my disciples indeed; and ye shall know the truth, and the truth shall make you free. They answered him, We be Abraham's seed, and were never in bondage to any man: how sayest thou, Ye shall be made free? Jesus answered them, Verily, verily, I say unto you, Whosoever committeth sin is the servant of sin. And the servant abideth not in the house for ever: but the Son abideth ever. If the Son therefore shall make you free, ye shall be free indeed." The service of God is not self-restraint, but self-indulgence. That is the first truth of all religion. That is the truth which we found uttered in those words of Jesus when we were thinking of them the other day. That is the truth to which we return as we come back again to think of those words and all that they mean and all that the speaker of them means to us and to our lives. When we remember that truth, when we recognize that no man is ever to be saved except by the fulfilment of his own nature, and not by the restraint of his nature, when we recognize that no man, no personal, individual man, is ever to be ransomed from his sins except by having opened to him a larger and fuller life into which he has entered, we seem to have displayed to us a large region, into which we are tempted to enter, and which is so rich and inviting to us that we immediately begin to ask ourselves if it is possible that there should be such a region. It is simply a great dream that we set before us. It is something that we imagine, something that comes out of the imaginations and anticipations of our own hearts, simply stimulated by the possibilities of the life in which we are living. It would be very much indeed, if it were only that. It would bear a certain testimony of itself, if it simply came out of the perpetual dissatisfaction of men's souls, even if there were no distinct manifestation of that life and no possibility of entering into it at once with our own personal consecration, with the resolution of our own wills. But if it were simply a dream, ultimately it must fade away out of the thoughts of men. It is impossible that men should keep on, year after year, age after age, this simple dream of something which does not exist. It would be like those pictures which the poet has drawn, something which appeals to nothing in our human nature and stands only as a parable of something that is a great deal lower than itself. The poet pictures to us in his imagination those things which do not appeal to our life, because they find nothing to correspond to their high portraits, to show those transformations of nature into something that is entirely different and foreign to itself. If religion be simply the dream that some men hold it to be, if it simply be the cheating of man's soul with that which has no reality to correspond to it, then it will be no more than this. Is there any assurance that is given to us, that is before the soul of man, of some great new life which it is given for man to seek, without which it is given for no man to be satisfied? I do not know where any man could find that assurance absolutely and entirely, unless there had stood forth before us the person of Him who spoke these words and who manifested them in His life. And therefore it is that, having pictured to you the richness of the life which is open to every man, his own true life, the large freedom into which he may go if, giving up his sins he enters into the fulness of the life of God, I cannot help now calling you to think about Him who gives, not merely by His words, but by the whole of His own person and life, that manifestation of the reality of the divine existence and tempts us to follow after Him. In other words, we come to-day to think of Christ, Christ who claims to be the master of the world, Christ from whom the revelation of that higher life has come, not in its first instance in the manifestation of the words which he spoke, for it had been the dream of human hearts through all the ages, but who made it so distinct and clear that ever since the time of Christ men have been able to cease to seek after it, men have never been able to give up the hope and dream that it was there. It is our Christ in whom we Christians believe. It is the Christ in whom a great many of you listening to me now claim to believe—I do myself—in whom many of you do believe, whom many of you have followed into that newer life. I would to God that I could so set Him before you to-day, could so make you feel his actual presence in the life which we are living, which we may be living, that there should be no question in any man of the power that is open before him to enter into the higher life and to fulfil his soul to God. What I want to do, in the few moments which I may speak to you this morning, is—laying aside all the theological conceptions regarding Him, laying aside everything that attaches to the complications and mysteries in which His nature has been involved in men's dreams of Him, laying aside everything which the churches are holding as the special doctrine of their especial creed—to go back to the very beginning and see if we can understand anything of what it is—this personal Christ, who lives here in the world and manifests the power of God and opens the possibility of every man. Surely it is good that we should know something about Him of whom we speak so much, that there should be some clear and directest conception of one whose name has been upon the lips of men for eighteen hundred years; and it is possible for us, in the simplest way, to understand how His power has come into the world and to see where it is possible that it should come and enrich our lives and make us different men. We go back, then, to the very beginning of the aspiration after God, which is in the heart of man everywhere. There has never been a race that has been without it. There has never been a generation that has not reached forward and thought there was a higher life, a fuller liberty, to which it could come. It has been in all the religions which have been not simply fears, but which have been the highest utterances of all the different races in all the different generations of mankind and all the different countries of the world; and there was one especial race in one especial part of the world in whom that aspiration was especially strong. We will not ask how it came to be there. There it was in this strange people living on the eastern shore of the Mediterranean Sea, and in all its history marked out by the strange peculiarity that it was a spiritual people, that in the midst of all its sins, blunders, and weaknesses it was forever lifting up its soul to God and striving to find Him out. Very often it blundered strangely and sadly. Very often it failed to get that for which it was seeking, by the very impetuousness, rashness, and earnestness of search. But it was always seeking after Him. And the years rolled by, and by and by in the midst of that great nation there was a little company of men who, accompanying one another from the beginning of their lives, had been searching after this God and trying everywhere if they could find Him. And one day they heard that down by the river which ran through their country, which was sacred to them from the multitude of old national associations, there was a great teacher come, who was declaring that for which the human soul was forever reaching after, the need of escaping from sin and entering upon and leading a higher life. This little company went down and met two disciples of John the Baptist, and learned from them everything that they had to teach them. Their souls were stirred by that which he had to say. But one day, while he was teaching them, it seemed as if they had come to an end of that which he could teach them. He looked up, and there upon the hill just above the river there was passing one upon whom the gaze of the fishermen by the river immediately kindled, and he lifted his hand and said, "He is the one who is to teach you now. You must go after him. Behold the Lamb of God, which taketh away the sin of the world." Great and mysterious words, that filled in that which men had believed in all the records they had read and the thinking they had done before! And they turned away from John and went after this new teacher and, following to His house, there they abode with Him during that day and the days that followed after. Little by little, as we read the story of their being with him, we can see them taken into His power, we can see how there was a certain fascination in His presence which laid hold upon them. It seemed at first to be purely human, to be the way in which one strong man takes possession of his fellow-man and compels him to rely upon him. It was upon purely human ground. It was in the manifestation of the excellence of this human nature of ours that they believed in Jesus and gradually became His disciples. Little by little it so commanded them that at last the moment came when it was impossible for them to separate themselves from Him; and one day, when the people were turning away from Him when He was preaching and saying things that it was hard for them to understand, He looked around upon them and said, "Are you going also, will you leave me now?" And then there burst forth from the lips of one of them, the most strong and characteristic act of the little company, those great words that declared how He had become necessary to them: "Lord, to whom shall we go? Thou hast the words of eternal life." You see the power that Jesus had acquired over these men. You see the way in which He had taken them absolutely into His dominion, simply because of the manifestation of character and life, simply because He had shown them what man might be and opened the springs of the better life in themselves by the words He had spoken to them. And then they lived on with Him still, and by and by they had become so convinced by His truth and wisdom, His character had so taken possession of them, that they were ready to believe anything that He said. One day He lifted up His voice and declared that which had gradually been dawning upon them all the time, that He was more than they were, that He had brought in some mysterious way a divine life into this world and had much to communicate to them. He told them that He was the Father from whom His life and their life had come. He told them that He and the Father were one. He told them, not in theological statement, not as men have worked out since in their desire to know it fully, but in the simple statement of the truth that could be the inspiration of their life, that in His presence there was here the very presence of God among them. It was not strange to them, though human creatures, though men, that the highest aspiration of their humanity had never thought God so far from this world that it seemed to them strange that there should be in very human presence the divine life here with them. They could not explain it and did not try to explain it. Here it was, that which they had seen shadowed in the divinest men whom they had known, that which they had recognized. Here it was before them in this being who had won such a power over them that they were ready to accept His testimony with regard to Himself. Oh! my friends, let us not feel that the evidence of our Christian faith fails when it is seen to rest upon the word of Christ Himself. My neighbor knows more of himself than I know of him. I know more of myself than any man can know of me, if only I be earnest and sincere. And that the greatest of men who ever trod this earth should not know more of His nature than any other man should know, and that therefore His word should not be the richest revelation of that which is in His life and makes His power over mankind, that is incredible. Therefore the men were right when they believed Jesus' own word and looked to Him for the divinity which He said was present with Him upon the earth. Then His life went on, and by and by fulfilled itself in the one great action in which He declared those two things which He longed to know, the life and newness of God and the power of their human nature. He gave His life for them, indeed, in the awful suffering that preceded and that culminated upon the cross. He gave

His life in crucifixion for them, and in that crucifixion opened the divinest doors of His life, when opening a sanctuary of sorrow; and He bade them enter in and know there the absolute life of God and the great capacity of human nature to sacrifice itself for God. And before He died, and afterward, He again appeared to them. He spoke great words which said that this was not the end of things, that after they had ceased to see Him and touch Him and hear His voice He still was to be present in the world. He said that the mysterious presence of those who had passed away, which all had known, was to culminate and be fulfilled in Him. "I am with you alway, even unto the end of the world." Wherever you "are together in my name, there am I." Words and words and words again like those He spoke, in which He declared that He was to be an everlasting presence among mankind, and therefore that which had taken place in the life of those disciples might forever take place; that that which Jesus had done in the days when He was present upon the earth should be continually repeated, in that He was forever to do that which He had been doing, giving Himself to human kind for their inspiration, for their elevation, for their correction, for their reproof, as He had been doing, their salvation, as He had been doing in those days in which He was here among them. Men have believed that simply. They have recognized that word of Christ, and found the fulfilment of it in their own lives; and that has been the Christian religion,—just exactly what it was in the old days when Jesus was present in Jerusalem and Galilee. Just exactly what men did then men have been doing in all the generations that have come since. Just exactly what was possible then is possible for them now—that we may become the followers of that same Christ and the receivers through Him of the divine life, by which alone the human life is perfected and fulfilled.

That is the Christian religion. That is the Christian faith. Is it not clear and simple, whether it be true or not? My friends, you may believe it or you may disbelieve it, but the Christian faith is clear and simple enough surely in this statement, stripped of a thousand difficulties, perplexities, and bewilderments. That is it, that there is in the world to-day the same Christ who was in the world eighteen hundred and more years ago, and that men may go to Him and receive His life and the inspiration of His presence and the guidance of His wisdom just exactly as they did then. If you and I had been in Jerusalem in those old days, what would we have done, if we were more than mere creatures of others, more than men merely absorbed in our business, if there were any stirring in our souls after the deeper and diviner desires, could we, would we have been satisfied until we had gone wherever He might be,—in the temple, in the courts, or on the country road,—and found that Jesus, and entered into some sympathy with His life, that He might give to us what revelation of life and what guidance of will it might be possible should come from Him to men who trusted Him, until we had entered into sympathy with Him and the fascinations of His character? That is the Christian life, my friends, the thing we make so vague and mysterious and difficult. That is the Christian life, the following of Jesus Christ.

What is the Christian? Everywhere the man who, so far as he comprehends Jesus Christ, so far as he can get any knowledge of Him, is His servant, the man who makes Christ a teacher of his intelligence and the guide of his soul, the man who obeys Christ as far as he has been able to understand Him. What, you say, the man who imperfectly understands Christ, who don't know anything about His divinity, who denies the great doctrines of the Church in regard to Him, is he a Christian? Certainly he is, my friends. There is no other test than this, the following of Jesus Christ. So far as any soul deeply consecrated to Him, and wanting the influence that it feels that He has to give, follows Christ, enters into His obedience and His company, and receives His blessings, just so far He is able to bestow it. I cannot sympathize with any feeling that desires to make the name of Christian a narrower name. I would spread it just as wide as it can be possibly made to spread. I would know any man as a Christian, rejoice to know any man as a Christian, whom Jesus would recognize as a Christian, and Jesus Christ, I am sure, in those old days recognized His followers even if they came after Him with the blindest sight, with the most imperfect recognition and acknowledgment of what He was and of what He could do.

And then, again, is it not very strange, certainly, that there should be, in these later days, in all these centuries that have passed between the day of Jesus Christ and us, that there should have come a vast accumulation of speculation and conjecture, of theorizing and thought with regard to Christ and what He was, and that a great deal of it should have been very strange and should seem to us to-day to have been very silly, a great part of it should have seemed to be but a work of intelligences that were half dulled and blinded, full of prejudice, and shrinking from the error and the danger in which they stood? What does it mean—all these complicated theologies that we say are keeping us away from the simple following of the grandest figure that has ever presented Himself before human kind? I know not how else it can be when I see what has been the power of Jesus over thoughts and homes and hearts of men through all these years. It seems to be a previous necessity that He who most fastens the heart and life of man, who seems to be most necessary to the soul of men, shall so attract their thought, shall so draw them all to Himself that their crudest speculations, that their most erroneous conceptions, shall fasten upon him, and they shall be in some true way a testimony of the way in which He has always held the human heart. This is the way in which all crudities of theology, all the weaknesses of speculation, all even of the most strange and foul thoughts in regard to the life of Jesus and His manifestation in the world, have accumulated around that gracious figure, so simple and strong, which walks through our human life and manifests to us the God. Surely it is in one conception of it, and the true conception of it, the great perpetual testimony of how men have cared about Jesus, that they have speculated about Him in such strange perplexing ways. But He about whom the world does not care walks through the world and bears His simple being. There is nothing that fastens upon Him, that perplexes His life, that makes mysterious and strange the life He lives. But where is the great man in all the history of human kind that has not gathered about his person and work the speculations of those whom we find, with their crude and unguided minds, have formed their theories in regard to Him? It is the very abundance of the strange speculations with regard to Christ, it is the very strangeness of the theories that have been formed with regard to Him, that has shown me how He has drawn the hearts of men, how He has not let them go, but compelled them to fasten themselves to Him, to think about Him and try to follow Him in such poor, blind ways as they were able to give themselves to Him in. This, then, is the Christian faith. This is the way in which the larger life opens before mankind, by the following of a person, by the giving of the life into the dominion and the guidance and the obedience of one who goes forward into that life, himself thoroughly believing in it—for Jesus believed in it with all His human soul.

But then, we ask ourselves, is it possible that we can gather from such a life as Jesus lived so long ago, a life that was lived back in the very dust of history and that has come down to us in records which seem sometimes to be flecked with tradition and obscured with the distance in which they lived, is it possible that I should get from him a guidance of my daily life here? Am I, a man of the nineteenth century, when everything has changed, in Boston, in this modern civilization,—can Jesus really be my teacher, my guide, in the actual duties and perplexities of my daily life and lead me into the larger land in which I know he lives? Ah! the man knows very little about the everlasting identity of human nature, little of how the world in all these changeless ages is the same, who asks that; very little, also, of how in every largest truth there are all particulars and details of human life involved; little of how everything that a man is to-day, upon every moment, rests upon some eternal foundation and may be within the power of some everlasting law. The wonder of the life of Jesus is this—and you will find it so and you have found it so if you have ever taken your New Testament and tried to make it the rule of your daily life—that there is not a single action that you are called upon to do of which you need be, of which you will be, in any serious doubt for ten minutes as to what Jesus Christ, if He were here, Jesus Christ being here, would have you do under those circumstances and with the material upon which you are called to act. Men have tried to go back and imitate the very activities of the life of Jesus Christ, to do the very things that He did. Souls have fled across the sea and tried upon the hills and in the plains where Jesus lived to reproduce the life that has so fascinated them. They were poor and unphilosophic souls. The soul that takes in Jesus' word, the soul that through the words of Jesus enters into the very person of Jesus, the soul that knows Him as its daily presence and its daily law—it never hesitates. Do I doubt—I, who see myself called upon to be the slave of these conditions which are around me—to do this thing? Because it is the custom of the business in which I am engaged, do I doubt fora moment if I turn aside and open this New Testament, which is Jesus' law with regard to that thing? I, with my passion boiling in my veins, leading me to do some foul act of outrageous lust, have I a single moment's doubt what Jesus would have me do if He were here—what Jesus, being here, really wants me to do? There is no single act of your life, my friend, there is no single dilemma in which you find yourself placed, in which the answer is not in Jesus Christ. I do not say that you will find some words in Jesus' teachings in the Gospel of Matthew, Mark, Luke, and John that will detail exactly the condition in which you find yourself placed; but I do say that if, with your human sympathies and your devoted love, you can feel the presence of that Jesus behind the words that He said, the personal perfectness, the divine life manifested in the human life, there is not a single sin or temptation to sin that will not be convicted.

There is where we rest when we claim that Jesus Christ is the master of the world, that He opens the great richness and infinite distances of the human life, that He shows us what it is to be men. It would be little if He did that simply with the painting of some glorious vision upon the skies beyond; but that He comes into your life and mine, into our homes and our shops, into our offices and on our streets, and there makes known in the actual circumstances of our daily life what we ought to do and what we ought not to do—that is the wonder of his revelation; that is what proclaims him to be the Son of God and the Son of man. Think, as you sit here, of anything that you are doing that is wrong, of any habit of your life, of your self-indulgence, or of that great, pervasive habit of your life which makes you a creature of the present instead of the eternities, a creature of the material earth instead of the glorious skies. Ask of yourself of any habit that belongs to your own personal life, and bring it face to face with Jesus Christ and see if it is not judged. A judgment day that is far away, that is off in the dim distance when this world is done—it shall come, no doubt. I know none of us can know much with regard to it, except that it is sure. But the judgment day that is here now is Christ; the judgment day that is right close to your life and rebukes you, if you will let Him rebuke you every time you sin, the judgment day that is here and praises you and bids you be of good courage, when you do a thing that men disown and despise, is Christ. Therefore it is no figure of speech, it is no mere ecstasy of the imagination of the preacher, when we say that in the midst of these streets of ours, more real than the men that walk in them, more real than the sidewalks that are under our feet, and the buildings that tower over us, there walks an unseen presence. An unseen presence? Yes. Are you and I going to be such creatures of our senses that we shall not believe that there are powers that touch us that we cannot see? Am I going to be so bound down to these poor fingers and to these poor eyes that I shall know myself in no larger connection with the great, unseen world? I will not. No great man, no manly man, has ever allowed such a limitation of himself. There is the unseen presence in the midst of our life, and he who will feel it may feel it, and that unseen presence speaks to him continually. It knows every one of us. It knows the rich man and knows what his wealth has made of him. It knows whether it has made him selfish. Shall I say it? He, the Christ, the present Christ, knows whether the rich man's riches have made him selfish and base and mean, covetous and poor and little-souled, or whether he has been glad to rise to the greatness of his privilege, and be the very utterance of the beneficence of God upon the earth. He knows the poor man and his struggles, he knows the poor man and his self-respect. He speaks to the poor man's soul, who has been kept poor because he will not enter into the baser methods and motives of our modern life, and is despised, and says to him, "Be of good courage, for I know what you are." He speaks to the poor in distress and poverty. He speaks to the wretched in their disappointment and their pain. He is their comforter. He knows every sin. He knows every sorrow of our life. He goes, unseen on earth, into the chambers where the dead lie dead, and where the sick lie dying, and He speaks His words of consolation, He opens up the glory of the perfect life. He lays his hand upon the mourner whose soul is bowed down to the earth and says, "Look up," and points into eternity and heaven. All these things Christ can do not merely, but Christ is doing. He is the inspiring power of this life, that keeps it from rotting in its corruption and degradation. We dwell too much, I think, upon some of these things; we cannot dwell too much, perhaps, but we dwell out of proportion, it may be, to the thought of Jesus Christ, the comforter of sorrow. He is the comforter of sorrow, for he knew and he knows what sorrow is. In His own crucifixion, in that which came before His crucifixion, He knew the suffering of this earthly life. There is no human being who ever has known the misery of man as Jesus knows it, and so He comes to all sorrows with tender consolation. God grant, God grant He may come to any of you who have come into these doors to-day with a sorrow, with a fear, with a dread upon your hearts, with souls that are wrung, with bodies that are suffering! God grant that the Christ may comfort you, may comfort you! But not only that. Shall there be no Christ for those who for the moment seem to need no comfort?

Shall there be no Christ for the strong men who have before them the duties of their life, and who want the strength with which to do them? Shall there be no Christ for the young men, the young men standing in danger, but also standing in such magnificent and splendid chances? It is great to think of Christ standing by the sorrowing and comforting them. It is great,—we will not say it is greater,—it is very great, when by the side of the young man just entering into life there stands the Christ, saying to his soul, with the voice that he cannot fail to hear: "Be pure, be strong, be wise, be independent; rejoice in Me and My appreciation. Let the world go, if it is necessary that the world should go. Serve the world, but do not be the servant of the world. Make the world your servant by helping the world in every way in which you can minister to its life. Be brave, be strong, be manly by My strength." Oh! young man, if you can hear the Christ speak to you like that behind all the traditions of the street, behind the teachings of the books, behind all that the wise and successful men say to you, behind all the cynics and sneerers say to you, the great, strong, healthy voice of Jesus Christ, who believes in man because He has known man filled with divinity, and believes in you because He knows that which has been set before you by your Father in the sending out of your life, and who longs and prays and waits to strengthen you, that you may do your work, that you may escape from sin, that you may live your life, this great figure of the present Christ that Christianity can produce—it is not the memory of something that is away back in the past, it is not the anticipation of something to come in the future. We talk about Christ the Saviour, and think about Calvary long ago. We talk about the Christ the Judge, and think of a great white throne set in some mystic valley of Jehoshaphat, where some day the world is to be judged. We do not so get hold of Christ. The Christ who is in the past is not our Christ unless His power holds forth, the power of

His spirit, which is the whole knowledge of the life in which we live. We think of the Christ of the future, for whom all the world is waiting. He will never enter into us and lead us unless we know that He is here and now. It does seem to me sometimes that if men would only take religion as a real and present thing, and if, instead of worshipping it in the past and expecting it with fear and dread and vain hope in the future, it could be a real thing with them here and now, something in which they are to live, not to which they are to flee in moments of doubt, not of which they should make rescue, but in which they should do all their work and live, then religion would be to the soul of man so that it could not be cast aside, so that they must enter into it and take it into themselves and make it their own. Religion is not the simple fire-escape that you build, in antici-pation of a possible danger, upon the outside of your dwelling and leave there until danger comes. You go to it some morning when a fire breaks out in your house, and the poor old thing that you built up there, and thought you could use some day, is so rusty and bro-ken, and the weather has so beaten upon it, and the sun so turned its hinges, that it will not work. That is the condition of a man who has built himself what seems to be a creed of faith, a trust in God in anticipation of the day when danger is to overtake him, and has said to himself, I am safe, for I will take refuge in it then. But reli-gion is the house in which we live, it is the table at which we sit, it is the fireside to which we draw near, the room that arches its graceful and familiar presence over us; it is the bed on which we lie and think of the past and anticipate the future and gather our refresh-ment. There is no Christ except the present Christ for every man, unto whom all the power of the historic Christ is always appearing, and who is great with all the sweet solemnity that comes from the knowledge of what in the future He is to be to the world and to the soul. I am anxious to-day to impress this upon you: that the Chris-tian faith is not a dogma, it is not primarily a law, but is a personal presence and an immediate life that is right here and now. I am anxious to have you know that to be a Christian does not mean primarily to believe this or that. It does not mean primarily, alt-hough it means necessarily afterward, to do this or that. But it means to know the presence of a true personal Christ among us and to follow. Here is the only true power by which a religion can be-come perpetual. Men outgrow many dogmas which they hold. The lines in which they try to live change their application to their lives. But I know a person with a deep, true life; I enter into a friendship with one who is worthy I should be his friend, and he is mine always. What is the meaning of this sort of talk that we hear about a faith that they held once, but they have outgrown? What is the reason of this expectation that seems to have spread itself abroad, of necessity that the boy who had a religion should lose his religion some time or other, and that by and by he should take up a man's religion somewhere upon the other side of the gulf of infidelity and godlessness, through which he has passed in the mean while? You expect your boy of ten years old to be religious with a child's sweet, trusting faith; and you hope that your man of forty and fifty, beaten by the world, is to have found a God who can be his salvation. But the years between? What do you think of your young men of fifteen, twenty, twenty-five, and thirty years old? To have outgrown the boy's faith, and not to have come to the man's faith? That seems almost to be an awful fate and destiny which you expect for them. But if our faith be this, then there shall be no need, no chance that a man shall outgrow it. Know Christ with the first conceptions, imperfect and crude, of his boy's life, and he shall go on knowing more and more of that Christ. That friend, the Christ he knows at twenty-five, shall be different from the Christ he knew at ten, just exactly as the friend I know at fifty is different from the friend I knew at thirty, twenty years ago; and yet He is the same friend still, forever opening the richness of an ever richer life, filling it with new experiences, with new manifestations of Himself. Let him drop something which seemed to him to be a part of the religion, but was only a temporary phase or condition of it, going forward with the soul all through the opening stages of life, and at last going forward with the soul into the life where it shall see as all along it has been seen, and know as it has been known. The old legend was that the clothes of the Israelites, which the Bible said waxed not old upon them in the desert during those forty years, not merely waxed not old those forty years, but grew with their growth, so that the little Hebrew who crossed the Red Sea in his boy's clothes wore the same clothes when he entered into the Promised Land. It is the parable of that which comes to the man who has a true Christian faith, a faith which comes in the personal friendship of Christ, a faith which comes not in the belief of certain things about Him, not in the doing slavishly of certain things which it seemed as if it had been said by Him that we must do, but in the personal entrance into His nature in a life for Him, in which He is able to send His life down into us.

Then there is another thing that people are always thinking, that I hear very often from men, and that I have no doubt that I should hear from many of you, one by one. You talk about your earlier religion as if it had been some sort of a bondage from which you had escaped. How common it is to hear men, especially in this region, say: "I would be, perhaps, religious, except that there was so much religion forced upon me in my earliest days. I was driven to church when I was a boy, in those old Puritan days. I went to school, where they forced prayers upon me all the time. I was made to be religious, so now I cannot be religious." Was there ever a more dreadful thing than for a soul to say that, because, it may be, of the unwisdom, or the imprudence, the overzeal and the mistaken zeal of other men, we have not got the full blessing of that rich, open, free life with Christ which the youth may have, and therefore we will abandon the privileges of our higher life which is given to us in our manlier years? It all comes of this awful way of talking as if religion were the duty and not the inestimable privilege of human kind. The Christ stands before us and says, "Come to me." You say, "Must I?" And He answers, "You may." He will not even say, "You must." You may. And duty loses itself in privilege, and the soul enters into independence and escapes from its sins, fulfils its life, lays hold of its salvation, becomes eternal, begins to live an eternal life in the accepted and loving service of Christ.

Now just one word, my friends. If this be so, whether you to-day are ready to make Christ your master and your friend or not, do not, I beg you, let yourself say that it is a silly or unreasonable belief, thus to know of a spiritual presence which is here among us, in which God is really in humanity. Do not let yourselves say, my friends, that the man who gives himself to Jesus Christ and earnestly tries to enter in deeper and deeper into his life and tries to do his will, that he may know the Christ and know himself in the Christ more and more — dare not call that brother a fool, as you have sometimes called your Christian man who watched scrupulously over his life and prayed, yes, prayed, the thing you think perhaps the foolishest thing that man can do, the thing that is the most reasonable act that any man does upon God's earth. If man is man and God is God, to live without prayer is not merely an awful thing: it is an infinitely foolish thing. When a man for the first time bows down upon his knees and prays, "Oh! Christ, come unto me, reveal Thyself to me, make me to know Thee, that I may receive Thee, make me to be obedient that I may take Thee into my life," then that man has claimed his manhood. I beg you, I implore you, I adjure you that, if you be not ready to be Christian, you at least will know that the Christian life is the only true human life, and that the man who becomes thoroughly a Christian sets his face toward the fulfilment of his humanity, and so for the first time truly is a man. "As many as received Him,"—so the great Scripture word runs of this Christ of whom we have been talking,—"As many as received Him, to them gave He power to become the sons of God."

Just think of it!—the sons of God! The power to become that to as many as will receive the present Christ.

# VI. ABRAHAM LINCOLN.[1]

"He chose David also His servant, and took him away from the sheepfolds; that he might feed Jacob His people, and Israel His inheritance. So he fed them with a faithful and true heart, and ruled them prudently with all his power."—PSALM lxxviii. 71, 72, 73.

While I speak to you to-day, the body of the President who ruled this people, is lying, honored and loved, in our city. It is impossible with that sacred presence in our midst for me to stand and speak of ordinary topics which occupy the pulpit. I must speak of him to-day; and I therefore undertake to do what I had intended to do at some future time, to invite you to study with me the character of Abraham Lincoln, the impulses of his life and the causes of his death. I know how hard it is to do it rightly, how impossible it is to do it worthily. But I shall speak with confidence, because I speak to those who love him, and whose ready love will fill out the deficiencies in a picture which my words will weakly try to draw.

We take it for granted, first of all, that there is an essential connection between Mr. Lincoln's character and his violent and bloody death. It is no accident, no arbitrary decree of Providence. He lived as he did, and he died as he did, because he was what he was. The more we see of events, the less we come to believe in any fate or destiny except the destiny of character. It will be our duty, then, to see what there was in the character of our great President that created the history of his life, and at last produced the catastrophe of his cruel death. After the first trembling horror, the first outburst of indignant sorrow, has grown calm, these are the questions which we are bound to ask and answer.

It is not necessary for me even to sketch the biography of Mr. Lincoln. He was born in Kentucky fifty-six years ago, when Kentucky was a pioneer State. He lived, as boy and man, the hard and needy life of a backwoodsman, a farmer, a river boatman, and, finally, by his own efforts at self-education, of an active, respected, influential citizen, in the half-organized and manifold interests of a new and energetic community. From his boyhood up he lived in direct and vigorous contact with men and things, not as in older States and easier conditions with words and theories; and both his moral convictions and his intellectual pinions gathered from that contact a supreme degree of that character by which men knew him, that character which is the most distinctive possession of the best American nature, that almost indescribable quality which we call in general clearness or truth, and which appears in the physical structure as health, in the moral constitution as honesty, in the mental structure as sagacity, and in the region of active life as practicalness. This one character, with many sides, all shaped by the same essential force and testifying to the same inner influences, was what was powerful in him and decreed for him the life he was to live and the death he was to die. We must take no smaller view than this of what he was. Even his physical conditions are not to be forgotten in making up his character. We make too little always of the physical; certainly we make too little of it here if we lose out of sight the strength and muscular activity, the power of doing and enduring, which the backwoods-boy inherited from generations of hard-living ancestors, and appropriated for his own by a long discipline of bodily toil. He brought to the solution of the question of labor in this country not merely a mind, but a body thoroughly in sympathy with labor, full of the culture of labor, bearing witness to the dignity and excellence of work in every muscle that work had toughened and every sense that work had made clear and true. He could not have brought the mind for his task so perfectly, unless he had first brought the body whose rugged and stubborn health was always contradicting to him the false theories of labor, and always asserting the true.

As to the moral and mental powers which distinguished him, all embraceable under this general description of clearness of truth, the most remarkable thing is the way in which they blend with one another, so that it is next to impossible to examine them in separation. A great many people have discussed very crudely whether Abraham Lincoln was an intellectual man or not; as if intellect were a thing always of the same sort, which you could precipitate from the other constituents of a man's nature and weigh by itself, and compare by pounds and ounces in this man with another. The fact is, that in all the simplest characters that line between the mental and moral natures is always vague and indistinct. They run together, and in their best combinations you are unable to discriminate, in the wisdom which is their result, how much is moral and how much is intellectual. You are unable to tell whether in the wise acts and words which issue from such a life there is more of the righteousness that comes of a clear conscience, or of the sagacity that comes of a clear brain. In more complex characters and under more complex conditions, the moral and the mental lives come to be less healthily combined. They co-operate, they help each other less. They come even to stand over against each other as antagonists; till we have that vague but most melancholy notion which pervades the life of all elaborate civilization, that goodness and greatness, as we call them, are not to be looked for together, till we expect to see and so do see a feeble and narrow conscientiousness on the one hand, and a bad, unprincipled intelligence on the other, dividing the suffrages of men.

It is the great boon of such characters as Mr. Lincoln's, that they reunite what God has joined together and man has put asunder. In him was vindicated the greatness of real goodness and the goodness of real greatness. The twain were one flesh. Not one of all the multitudes who stood and looked up to him for direction with such a loving and implicit trust can tell you to-day whether the wise judgments that he gave came most from a strong head or a sound heart. If you ask them, they are puzzled. There are men as good as he, but they do bad things. There are men as intelligent as he, but they do foolish things. In him goodness and intelligence combined and made their best result of wisdom. For perfect truth consists not merely in the right constituents of character, but in their right and intimate conjunction. This union of the mental and moral into a life of admirable simplicity is what we most admire in children; but in them it is unsettled and unpractical. But when it is preserved into manhood, deepened into reliability and maturity, it is that glorified childlikeness, that high and reverend simplicity, which shames and baffles the most accomplished astuteness, and is chosen by God to fill his purposes when he needs a ruler for his people, of faithful and true heart, such as he had who was our President.

Another evident quality of such a character as this will be its freshness or newness; if we may so speak. Its freshness or readiness—call it what you will—its ability to take up new duties and do them in a new way, will result of necessity from its truth and clearness. The simple natures and forces will always be the most pliant ones. Water bends and shapes itself to any channel. Air folds and adapts itself to each new figure. They are the simplest and the most infinitely active things in nature. So this nature, in very virtue of its simplicity, must be also free, always fitting itself to each new need. It will always start from the most fundamental and eternal conditions, and work in the straightest even although they be the newest ways, to the present prescribed purpose. In one word, it must be broad and independent and radical. So that freedom and radicalness in the character of Abraham Lincoln were not separate qualities, but the necessary results of his simplicity and childlikeness and truth.

Here then we have some conception of the man. Out of this character came the life which we admire and the death which we lament to-day. He was called in that character to that life and death. It was just the nature, as you see, which a new nation such as ours ought to produce. All the conditions of his birth, his youth, his manhood, which made him what he was, were not irregular and exceptional, but were the normal conditions of a new and simple country. His pioneer home in Indiana was a type of the pioneer land in which he lived. If ever there was a man who was a part of the time and country he lived in, this was he. The same simple respect for labor won in the school of work and incorporated into blood and muscle; the same unassuming loyalty to the simple virtues of temperance and industry and integrity; the same sagacious judgment which had learned to be quick-eyed and quick-brained in the constant presence of emergency; the same direct and clear thought about things, social, political, and religious, that was in him supremely, was in the people he was sent to rule. Surely, with such a type-man for ruler, there would seem to be but a smooth and even road over which he might lead the people whose character he represented into the new region of national happiness and comfort and usefulness, for which that character had been designed.

But then we come to the beginning of all trouble. Abraham Lincoln was the type-man of the country, but not of the whole country. This character which we have been trying to describe was the character of an American under the discipline of freedom. There was another American character which had been developed under the influence of slavery. There was no one American character embracing the land. There were two characters, with impulses of irrepressible and deadly conflict. This citizen whom we have been honoring and praising represented one. The whole great scheme with which he was ultimately brought in conflict, and which has finally killed him, represented the other. Beside this nature, true and fresh and new, there was another nature, false and effete and old. The one nature found itself in a new world, and set itself to discover the new ways for the new duties that were given it. The other nature, full of the false pride of blood, set itself to reproduce in a new world the institutions and the spirit of the old, to build anew the structure of the feudalism which had been corrupt in its own day, and which had been left far behind by the advancing conscience and needs of the progressing race. The one nature magnified labor, the other nature depreciated and despised it. The one honored the laborer, and the other scorned him. The one was simple and direct; the other, complex, full of sophistries and self-excuses. The one was free to look all that claimed to be truth in the face, and separate the error from the truth that might be in it; the other did not dare to investigate, because its own established prides and systems were dearer to it than the truth itself, and so even truth went about in it doing the work of error. The one was ready to state broad principles, of the brotherhood of man, the universal fatherhood and justice of God, however imperfectly it might realize them in practice; the other denied even the principles, and so dug deep and laid below its special sins the broad foundation of a consistent, acknowledged sinfulness. In a word, one nature was full of the influences of Freedom, the other nature was full of the influences of Slavery.

In general, these two regions of our national life were separated by a geographical boundary. One was the spirit of the North, the other was the spirit of the South. But the Southern nature was by no means all a Southern thing. There it had an organized, established form, a certain definite, established institution about which it clustered. Here, lacking advantage, it lived in less expressive ways and so lived more weakly. There, there was the horrible sacrament of slavery, the outward and visible sign round which the inward and spiritual temper gathered and kept itself alive. But who doubts that among us the spirit of slavery lived and thrived? Its formal existence had been swept away from one State after another, partly on conscientious, partly on economical grounds, but its spirit was here, in every sympathy that Northern winds carried to the listening ear of the Southern slave-holder, and in every oppression of the weak by the strong, every proud assumption of idleness over labor which echoed the music of Southern life back to us. Here in our midst lived that worse and falser nature, side by side with the true and better nature which God meant should be the nature of Americans, of which he was shaping out the type and champion in his chosen David of the sheepfold.

Here then we have the two. The history of our country for many years is the history of how these two elements of American life approached collision. They wrought their separate reactions on each other. Men debate and quarrel even now about the rise of Northern Abolitionism, about whether the Northern Abolitionists were right or wrong, whether they did harm or good. How vain the quarrel is! It was inevitable. It was inevitable in the nature of things that two such natures living here together should be set violently against each other. It is inevitable, till man be far more unfeeling and untrue to his convictions than he has always been, that a great wrong asserting itself vehemently should arouse to no less vehement assertion the opposing right. The only wonder is that there was not more of it. The only wonder is that so few were swept away to take by an impulse they could not resist their stand of hatred to the wicked institution. The only wonder is, that only one brave, reckless man came forth to cast himself, almost single-handed, with a hopeless hope, against the proud power that he hated, and trust to the influence of a soul marching on into the history of his countrymen to stir them to a vindication of the truth he loved. At any rate, whether the Abolitionists were wrong or right, there grew up about their violence, as there always will about the extremism of extreme reformers, a great mass of feeling, catching their spirit and asserting it firmly, though in more moderate degrees and methods. About the nucleus of Abolitionism grew up a great American Anti-Slavery determination, which at last gathered strength enough to take its stand to insist upon the checking and limiting the extension of the power of slavery, and to put the type-man, whom God had been preparing for the task, before the world, to do the work on which it had resolved. Then came discontent, secession, treason. The two American natures, long advancing to encounter, met at last, and a whole country, yet trembling with the shock, bears witness how terrible the meeting was.

Thus I have tried briefly to trace out the gradual course by which God brought the character which He designed to be the controlling character of this new world into distinct collision with the hostile character which it was to destroy and absorb, and set it in the person of its type-man in the seat of highest power. The character formed under the discipline of Freedom and the character formed under the discipline of Slavery developed all their difference and met in hostile conflict when this war began. Notice, it was not only in what he did and was towards the slave, it was in all he did and was everywhere that we accept Mr. Lincoln's character as the true result of our free life and institutions. Nowhere else could have come forth that genuine love of the people, which in him no one could suspect of being either the cheap flattery of the demagogue or the abstract philanthropy of the philosopher, which made our President, while he lived, the centre of a great household land, and when he died so cruelly, made every humblest household thrill with a sense of personal bereavement which the death of rulers is not apt to bring. Nowhere else than out of the life of freedom could have come that personal unselfishness and generosity which made so gracious a part of this good man's character. How many soldiers feel yet the pressure of a strong hand that clasped theirs once as they lay sick and weak in the dreary hospital! How many ears will never lose the thrill of some kind word he spoke—he who could speak so kindly to promise a kindness that always matched his word! How often he surprised the land with a clemency which made even those who questioned his policy love him the more for what they called his weakness,—seeing how the man in whom God had most embodied the discipline of Freedom not only could not be a slave, but could not be a tyrant! In the heartiness of his mirth and his enjoyment of simple joys; in the directness and shrewdness of perception which constituted his wit; in the untired, undiscouraged faith in human nature which he always kept; and perhaps above all in the plainness and quiet, unostentatious earnestness and independence of his religious life, in his humble love and trust of God—in all, it was a character such as only Freedom knows how to make.

Now it was in this character, rather than in any mere political position, that the fitness of Mr. Lincoln to stand forth in the struggle of the two American natures really lay. We are told that he did not come to the Presidential chair pledged to the abolition of Slavery. When will we learn that with all true men it is not what they intend to do, but it is what the qualities of their natures bind them to do, that determines their career! The President came to his power full of the blood, strong in the strength of Freedom. He came there free, and hating slavery. He came there, leaving on record words like these spoken three years before and never contradicted. He had said, "A house divided against itself cannot stand. I believe this Government cannot endure permanently, half slave and half free. I do not expect the Union to be dissolved; I do not expect the house to fall; but I expect it will cease to be divided. It will become all one thing or all the other." When the question came, he knew which thing he meant that it should be. His whole nature settled that question for him. Such a man must always live as he used to say he lived (and was blamed for saying it) "controlled by events, not controlling them." And with a reverent and clear mind, to be controlled by events means to be controlled by God. For such a man there was no hesitation when God brought him up face to face with Slavery and put the sword into his hand and said, "Strike it down dead." He was a willing servant then. If ever the face of a man writing solemn words glowed with a solemn joy, it must have been the face of Abraham Lincoln, as he bent over the page where the Emancipation Proclamation of 1863 was growing into shape, and giving manhood and freedom as he wrote it to hundreds of thousands of his fellow-men. Here was a work in which his whole nature could rejoice. Here was an act that crowned the whole culture of his life. All the past, the free boyhood in the woods, the free youth upon the farm, the free manhood in the honorable citizen's employments—all his freedom gathered and completed itself in this. And as the swarthy multitudes came in, ragged, and tired, and hungry, and ignorant, but free forever from anything but the memorial scars of the fetters and the whip, singing rude songs in which the new triumph of freedom struggled and heaved below the sad melody that had been shaped for bondage; as in their camps and hovels there grew up to their half-superstitious eyes the image of a great Father almost more than man, to whom they owed their freedom, — were they not half right? For it was not to one man, driven by stress of policy, or swept off by a whim of pity, that the noble act was due. It was to the American nature, long kept by God in his own intentions till his time should come, at last emerging into sight and power, and bound up and embodied in this best and most American of all Americans, to whom we and those poor frightened slaves at last might look up together and love to call him, with one voice, our Father.

Thus, we have seen something of what the character of Mr. Lincoln was, and how it issued in the life he lived. It remains for us to see how it resulted also in the terrible death which has laid his murdered body here in our town among lamenting multitudes to-day. It is not a hard question, though it is sad to answer. We saw the two natures, the nature of Slavery and the nature of Freedom, at last set against each other, come at last to open war. Both fought, fought long, fought bravely; but each, as was perfectly natural, fought with the tools and in the ways which its own character had made familiar to it. The character of Slavery was brutal, barbarous, and treacherous; and so the whole history of the slave power during the war has been full of ways of warfare brutal, barbarous, and treacherous, beyond anything that men bred in freedom could have been driven to by the most hateful passions. It is not to be marvelled at. It is not to be set down as the special sin of the war. It goes back beyond that. It is the sin of the system. It is the barbarism of Slavery. When Slavery went to war to save its life, what wonder if its barbarism grew barbarous a hundred-fold!

One would be attempting a task which once was almost hopeless, but which now is only needless, if he set himself to convince a Northern congregation that Slavery was a barbarian institution. It would be hardly more necessary to try to prove how its barbarism has shown itself during this war. The same spirit which was blind to the wickedness of breaking sacred ties, of separating man and wife, of beating women till they dropped down dead, of organizing licentiousness and sin into commercial systems, of forbidding knowledge and protecting itself with ignorance, of putting on its arms and riding out to steal a State at the beleaguered ballot-box away from freedom—in one word (for its simplest definition is its worst dishonor), the spirit that gave man the ownership in man in time of peace, has found out yet more terrible barbarisms for the time of war. It has hewed and burned the bodies of the dead. It has starved and mutilated its helpless prisoners. It has dealt by truth, not as men will in a time of excitement, lightly and with frequent violations, but with a cool, and deliberate, and systematic contempt. It has sent its agents into Northern towns to fire peaceful hotels where hundreds of peaceful men and women slept. It has undermined the prisons where its victims starved, and made all ready to blow with one blast their wretched life away. It has delighted in the lowest and basest scurrility even on the highest and most honorable lips. It has corrupted the graciousness of women and killed out the truth of men.

I do not count up the terrible catalogue because I like to, nor because I wish to stir your hearts to passion. Even now, you and I have no right to indulge in personal hatred to the men who did these things. But we are not doing right by ourselves, by the President that we have lost, or by God who had a purpose in our losing him, unless we know thoroughly that it was this same spirit which we have seen to be a tyrant in peace and a savage in war, that has crowned itself with the working of this final woe. It was the conflict of the two American natures, the false and the true. It was Slavery and Freedom that met in their two representatives, the assassin and the President; and the victim of the last desperate struggle of the dying Slavery lies dead to-day in Independence Hall.

Solemnly, in the sight of God, I charge this murder where it belongs, on Slavery. I dare not stand here in His sight, and before Him or you speak doubtful and double-meaning words of vague repentance, as if we had killed our President. We have sins enough, but we have not done this sin, save as by weak concessions and timid compromises we have let the spirit of Slavery grow strong and ripe for such a deed. In the barbarism of Slavery the foul act and its foul method had their birth. By all the goodness that there was in him; by all the love we had for him (and who shall tell how great it was); by all the sorrow that has burdened down this desolate and dreadful week,—I charge this murder where it belongs, on Slavery. I bid you to remember where the charge belongs, to write it on the door-posts of your mourning houses, to teach it to your wondering children, to give it to the history of these times, that all times to come may hate and dread the sin that killed our noblest President.

If ever anything were clear, this is the clearest. Is there the man alive who thinks that Abraham Lincoln was shot just for himself; that it was that one man for whom the plot was laid? The gentlest, kindest, most indulgent man that ever ruled a State! The man who knew not how to speak a word of harshness or how to make a foe! Was it he for whom the murderer lurked with a mere private hate? It was not he, but what he stood for. It was Law and Liberty, it was Government and Freedom, against which the hate gathered and the treacherous shot was fired. And I know not how the crime of him who shoots at Law and Liberty in the crowded glare of a great theatre differs from theirs who have levelled their aim at the same great beings from behind a thousand ambuscades and on a hundred battle-fields of this long war. Every general in the field, and every false citizen in our midst at home, who has plotted and labored to destroy the lives of the soldiers of the Republic, is brother to him who did this deed. The American nature, the American truths, of which our President was the anointed and supreme embodiment, have been embodied in multitudes of heroes who marched unknown and fell unnoticed in our ranks. For them, just as for him, character decreed a life and a death. The blood of all of them I charge on the same head. Slavery armed with Treason was their murderer.

Men point out to us the absurdity and folly of this awful crime. Again and again we hear men say, "It was the worst thing for themselves they could have done. They have shot a representative man, and the cause he represented grows stronger and sterner by his death. Can it be that so wise a devil was so foolish here? Must it not have been the act of one poor madman, born and nursed in his own reckless brain?" My friends, let us understand this matter. It was a foolish act. Its folly was only equalled by its wickedness. It was a foolish act. But when did sin begin to be wise? When did wickedness learn wisdom? When did the fool stop saying in his heart, "There is no God," and acting godlessly in the absurdity of his impiety? The cause that Abraham Lincoln died for shall grow stronger by his death,—stronger and sterner. Stronger to set its pillars deep into the structure of our nation's life; sterner to execute the justice of the Lord upon his enemies. Stronger to spread its arms and grasp our whole land into freedom; sterner to sweep the last poor ghost of Slavery out of our haunted homes. But while we feel the folly of this act, let not its folly hide its wickedness. It was the wickedness of Slavery putting on a foolishness for which its wickedness and that alone is responsible, that robbed the nation of a President and the people of a father. And remember this, that the folly of the Slave power in striking the representative of Freedom, and thinking that thereby it killed Freedom itself, is only a folly that we shall echo if we dare to think that in punishing the representatives of Slavery who did this deed, we are putting Slavery to death. Dispersing armies and hanging traitors, imperatively as justice and necessity may demand them both, are not killing the spirit out of which they sprang. The traitor must die because he has committed treason. The murderer must die because he has committed murder. Slavery must die, because out of it, and it alone, came forth the treason of the traitor and the murder of the murderer. Do not say that it is dead. It is not, while its essential spirit lives. While one man counts another man his born inferior for the color of his skin, while both in North and South prejudices and practices, which the law cannot touch, but which God hates, keep alive in our people's hearts the spirit of the old iniquity, it is not dead. The new American nature must supplant the old. We must grow like our President, in his truth, his independence, his religion, and his wide humanity. Then the character by which he died shall be in us, and by it we shall live. Then peace shall come that knows no war, and law that knows no treason; and full of his spirit a grateful land shall gather round his grave, and in the daily psalm of prosperous and righteous living, thank God forever for his life and death.

So let him lie here in our midst to-day, and let our people go and bend with solemn thoughtfulness and look upon his face and read the lessons of his burial. As he paused here on his journey from the Western home and told us what by the help of God he meant to do, so let him pause upon his way back to his Western grave and tell us with a silence more eloquent than words how bravely, how truly, by the strength of God, he did it. God brought him up as he brought David up from the sheepfolds to feed Jacob, his people, and Israel, his inheritance. He came up in earnestness and faith, and he goes back in triumph. As he pauses here to-day, and from his cold lips bids us bear witness how he has met the duty that was laid on him, what can we say out of our full hearts but this—"He fed them with a faithful and true heart, and ruled them prudently with all his power." The *Shepherd of the People*! that old name that the best rulers ever craved. What ruler ever won it like this dead President of ours? He fed us faithfully and truly. He fed us with counsel when we were in doubt, with inspiration when we sometimes faltered, with caution when we would be rash, with calm, clear, trustful cheerfulness through many an hour when our hearts were dark. He fed hungry souls all over the country with sympathy and consolation. He spread before the whole land feasts of great duty and devotion and patriotism, on which the land grew strong. He fed us with solemn, solid truths. He taught us the sacredness of government, the wickedness of treason. He made our souls glad and vigorous with the love of liberty that was in his. He showed us how to love truth and yet be charitable—how to hate wrong and all oppression, and yet not treasure one personal injury or insult. He fed *all* his people, from the highest to the lowest, from the most privileged down to the most enslaved. Best of all, he fed us with a reverent and genuine religion. He spread before us the love and fear of God just in that shape in which we need them most, and out of his faithful service of a higher Master who of us has not taken and eaten and grown strong? "He fed them with a faithful and true heart." Yes, till the last. For at the last, behold him standing with hand reached out to feed the South with mercy and the North with charity, and the whole land with peace, when the Lord who had sent him called him and his work was done!

He stood once on the battle-field of our own State, and said of the brave men who had saved it words as noble as any countryman of ours ever spoke. Let us stand in the country he has saved, and which is to be his grave and monument, and say of Abraham Lincoln what he said of the soldiers who had died at Gettysburg. He stood there with their graves before him, and these are the words he said: —

"We cannot dedicate, we cannot consecrate, we cannot hallow this ground. The brave men who struggled here have consecrated it far beyond our power to add or detract. The world will little note nor long remember what we say here, but it can never forget what they did here. It is for us the living rather to be dedicated to the unfinished work which they who fought here have thus far so nobly advanced. It is rather for us to be here dedicated to the great task remaining before us, that from these honored dead we take increased devotion to that cause for which they gave the last full measure of devotion; that we here highly resolve that these dead shall not have died in vain; and this nation, under God, shall have a new birth of freedom, and that government of the people, by the people, and for the people shall not perish from the earth."

May God make us worthy of the memory of Abraham Lincoln!

**FOOTNOTES:**

[Footnote 1: A sermon preached in Philadelphia, while the body of the
President was lying in the city.]